Incidents at the Shrine

Ben Okri is a Nigerian writer resident in London. He has published two novels, *Flowers and Shadows* and *The Landscapes Within*. He studied at the University of Essex and has had short stories published in the *New Statesman*, *Firebird* and *PEN New Fiction*. He is poetry editor of the magazine *West Africa* and has worked as a broadcaster with the BBC. In 1984 he was awarded an Arts Council bursary, and he is currently working on a new novel.

Books by Ben Okri

Flowers and Shadows
The Landscapes Within

Ben Okri

Incidents at the Shrine

SHORT STORIES

Flamingo
Published by Fontana Paperbacks

First published in Great Britain by
William Heinemann Ltd 1986

This Flamingo edition first published
in 1987 by Fontana Paperbacks,
8 Grafton Street, London W1X 3LA

Flamingo is an imprint of
Fontana Paperbacks, part of
the Collins Publishing Group

'Laughter Beneath the Bridge' was first published
in *Firebird* 4. 'A Hidden History' appeared in the
New Statesman. An early fragment of 'Converging City'
was published in *West Africa*. 'Disparities' was
published in *PEN New Fiction 1*.

Made and printed in Great Britain by
William Collins Sons & Co. Ltd, Glasgow

To R.C.

When you have finished
And done up my stitches,
Wake me near the altar,
And this poem will be finished.

Christopher Okigbo

Contents

Laughter Beneath the Bridge   1

Converging City   23

Disparities   37

Incidents at the Shrine   53

Masquerades   67

A Hidden History   81

Crooked Prayer   91

The Dream-vendor's August   105

Laughter Beneath the Bridge

T HOSE WERE LONG days as we lay pressed to the prickly grass waiting for the bombs to fall. The civil war broke out before mid-term and the boarding school emptied fast. Teachers disappeared; the English headmaster was rumoured to have flown home; and the entire kitchen staff fled before the first planes went past overhead. At the earliest sign of trouble in the country parents appeared and secreted away their children. Three of us were left behind. We all hoped someone would turn up to collect us. We were silent most of the time.

Vultures showed up in the sky. They circled the school campus for a few days and then settled on the watch-night's shed. In the evenings we watched as some religious maniacs roamed the empty school compound screaming about the end of the world and then as a wild bunch of people from the city scattered through searching for those of the rebel tribe. They broke doors and they looted the chapel of its icons, statuaries and velvet drapes; they took the large vivid painting of the agony of Christ. In the morning we saw the Irish priest riding furiously away from town on his Raleigh bicycle. After he left, ghosts flitted through the chapel and rattled the roof. One night we heard the altar fall. The next day we saw lizards nodding on the chapel walls.

We stayed on in the dormitories. We rooted for food in the vegetable field. We stole the wine of tapsters at the foot of palm trees. We broke into the kitchen and raided the store of baked beans, sardines and stale bread. In the daytime we waited at the school gate, pressed to the grass, watching out for our parents. Sometimes we went to town to forage. We talked about the bombings in the country whispered to us from the fields. One day, after having stolen bread from the only bakery open in town, we got to the dormitory and found the lizards there. They were under the double-decked beds and on the cupboards, in such great numbers, in such relaxed occupation, that we couldn't bear to sleep there any more. All through the days we waited for the bombs to fall. And all through that time it was Monica I thought about.

She was a little girl when I learned how to piss straight. When I learned how to cover my nakedness she developed long legs and a pert behind and took to moving round our town like a wild and beautiful cat. She became famous for causing havoc at the barbers' shops, the bukkas, pool offices. She nearly drowned once trying to outswim the other boys across our town's river, which was said to like young girls. I watched them dragging her through the muddied water: her face was pale, she looked as though she had taken a long journey from her body. After that she took to going around with Egun-guns, brandishing a whip, tugging the masked figure, abusing the masquerade for not dancing well enough. That was a time indeed when she broke our sexual taboos and began dancing our street's Egungun round town, fooling all the men. She danced so well that we got coins from the stingiest dressmakers, the meanest pool-shop owners. I remember waking up one night during the holidays to go out and ease myself at the backyard. I saw her bathing near the shrub of hibiscus; and there was a moon out. I dreamed of her new-formed breasts when the lizards chased us from the dormitories, and when the noise of fighter planes drove us to the forests.

I remember it as a beautiful time: I don't know how. Sirens and fire engines made it seem like there was an insane feast going on somewhere in the country. In town we saw a man set upon by a mob: they beat him up in a riot of vengeance, they broke sticks and bottles on his head. So much blood came from him. Maybe it seemed like a beautiful time because we often sat in the school field, staring at the seven hills that were like pilings of verdigris in the distance: and because none of us cried. We were returning from a search for food one day when we saw someone standing like a scarecrow in the middle of the field. We drew closer. The figure stayed still. It was mother. She looked at us a long time and she didn't recognize me. Fear makes people so stiff. When she finally recognized me she held all three of us together like we were a family.

'Can't take your friends,' mother said, after we had all been given something to eat.

'I'm not a wicked person to leave behind children who are stranded,' mother said, her face bony, 'but how will I rest in my grave if the soldiers we meet hold them, because of me?'

I didn't understand. I began to say a prayer for my friends.

'You will have to wait for your parents, or both of you go with the first parent that turns up. Can you manage?' mother asked them. They nodded. She looked at them for a long time and then cried.

Mother left them some money and all the food she brought. She took off two of her three wrappers for them to cover themselves with in the cold winds of the night. I felt sad at having to leave them behind. Mother prayed for them and I tried not to think of them as we walked the long distance to the garage. I tried not to see both of them in the empty fields as we struggled to catch a bus in the garage. Then the commotion of revving lorries, wheezing buses, the convulsion of people running home to their villages, women weeping, children bawling, soldiers everywhere in battle-dress and camouflage helmets, their guns stiff and strange, the whole infernal commotion simply wiped my two friends from my mind. After several hours we finally caught a lorry that could take us home. Then afterwards I tried to think only of Monica.

The lorry we caught was old and slow. It had an enduring, asthmatic engine. The driver was very talkative and boastful. There were all kinds of cupboards and long brooms and things in sacks strapped to its roof. As we fought to clamber in, I caught a glimpse of the legend painted on the old wooden bodywork. It read: THE YOUNG SHALL GROW.

There was absolutely no space in the lorry to move because most of the passengers had brought with them as many of the acquisitions of their lives in the city as they could carry. We sat on wooden benches and all about us were buckets, sewing machines, mattresses, calabashes, mats, clothes, ropes, pots, blackened pans, machetes. Even those with household jujus could not hide them: and we stared at the strange things they worshipped. It was so uncomfortable and airless in the lorry that I nodded in and out of sleep, the only relief.

That was a long journey indeed. The road seemed to have no end. The leaves of the trees and bushes were covered with dust. There were a hundred checkpoints. The soldiers at every one of them seemed possessed of a belligerent vitality. They stopped every vehicle, searched all nooks and crannies, emptied every bag and sack, dug their guns in our behinds, barked a thousand questions. We passed stretches of forest and saw numerous corpses along the road. We saw whole families trudging along the empty wastes, children straggling behind, weeping without the possibility of consolation.

I was asleep when mother woke me up. It was another checkpoint. There were many soldiers around, all shouting and barking orders at the same time. There was a barricade across the road. There was a pit not far from the barricade. The bodies of three grown men lay bundled in the pit. One of them had been shot through the teeth. Another one was punctured with gunshots and his face was so contorted it seemed he had died from too much laughing.

The soldiers shouted that we should all jump down. It would begin all over again: unpacking the entire lorry, unstrapping the load at the top, being subjected to a thorough and leisurely search. Then we would wait for one or two who couldn't prove they were not of the rebel tribe, sometimes being made to leave without them.

'Come down, all of you! Jump down now!' shouted the soldiers. We all tramped down. They lined us up along the road. Evening was approaching and the sun had that ripe, insistent burn. The forest was riotous with insects. Many of the soldiers had their fingers on the triggers. As they searched the lorry, one of the soldiers kept blowing his nose, covering the lemon-grass with snot. They questioned the driver, who shivered in servility. They took us aside, into the bush, one by one, to be questioned. I stood there beneath the mature burning sun, starving, bored, and thinking of Monica. Occasionally I heard one of the women burst into crying. I heard the butt of a gun crash on someone's head. I didn't hear them cry out.

They searched and questioned us a long time. The sun turned from ripe, blazing red to dull orange. I blew my nose on the lemon-grass, thinking of Monica. The soldier who had also been blowing his nose came over to me.

'You dey crase?' he shouted at me.

I didn't know what he was talking about so he cracked me across the head. I saw one of Monica's masks in the stars.

'Are you mad?' he shouted at me again.

I still didn't know what he was talking about. He whacked me harder, with the back of his hand, and sent me flying into the cluster of yellowing lemon-grass. Mother screamed at him, dived for his eyes, and he pushed her so hard that she landed near me. She picked herself up, snot drooling from the back of her wrapper; her wig had fallen into the pit. I lay on the lemon-grass and refused to get up. My head hurt. Behind me another soldier was knocking a woman about in the bushes. The soldier who had hit me came over to where I lay. His gun pointed at me from the hip. Mother, who feared guns, cowered behind him. Someone called to the soldier.

'Frank O'Nero,' the voice said, 'leave the poor boy alone now, ah ah.'

Frank O'Nero turned to the voice, swinging the gun in its direction, then swinging back to me. His eyes were raw. I was afraid that he was mad.

'All you children of rich men. You think because you go to school you can behave anyhow you want? Don't you know this is war? Goat! Small goat!'

Mother, in a weak voice, said: 'Leave my son alone, you hear. God didn't give me many of them.'

Frank O'Nero looked at her, then at me. He turned with a swagger and went to the bush where they were questioning the passengers. They called us next.

Behind the bushes three soldiers smoked marijuana. Half-screened, a short way up, two soldiers struggled with a light-complexioned woman. The soldiers smoking marijuana asked mother questions and I never heard her answers because I was fascinated with what the soldiers a short way up were doing. The soldiers asked mother where she came from in the country and I thought of Monica as the soldiers, a short way up, struggled with and finally subdued the woman. They shouted to mother to recite the paternoster in the language of the place she claimed to come from: and mother hesitated as the woman's legs were forced apart. Then mother recited the paternoster fluently in father's language. She was of the rebel tribe but father had long ago forced her to master his language. Mother could tell that the interpreter who was supposed to check on the language didn't know it too well: so she extended the prayer, went deeper into idiom, abusing their mothers and fathers, cursing the suppurating vaginas that must have shat them out in their wickedness, swearing at the rotten pricks that dug up the maggoty entrails of their mothers – and the soldiers half-screened by the bushes rode the woman furiously till the sun started its slow climb into your eyes, Monica. The soldiers listened to mother's recitation with some satisfaction. Then they turned to me and asked me to recite the Hail Mary. The soldier in the bush had finished wrecking his manhood on the woman and was cleaning himself with leaves. I told the soldier interrogating me that I couldn't speak our language that well.

'Why not?' he asked, his voice thundering.

I heard the question but couldn't find an answer.

The woman on the floor in the bush was silent: her face was contorted, she was covered in a foam of sweat.

'I'm talking to you! Idiot!' he shouted. 'If you don't speak your language you're not going with your mother, you hear?'

I nodded. Their marijuana smoke was beginning to tickle me. Mother came in quickly and explained that I hadn't grown up at home. The woman on the ground began to wail tonelessly. Mother turned on me, pinched me, hit my head, urged me to speak the language of my father, gave me hints of children's songs, the beginnings of stories. I couldn't at that moment remember a word: it had all simply vanished from my head. Besides, I was suddenly overcome with the desire to laugh.

It was partly the interrogator's fault. He said: 'If he can't speak a word of your language then he can't be your son.'

I burst out laughing and not even mother's pincerous fingernails, nor the growing fury of the soldiers, could stop me. I soon found myself being dragged deep into the forest by Frank O'Nero. Mother wailed a dirge, her hair all scattered. The woman on the ground made inhuman noises. Fear overcame me and I shouted the oldest word I knew and mother seized on it, screaming, the boy has spoken, he has just said that he wants to shit. Frank O'Nero stopped, his fingers like steel round my wrists. He looked at the other soldiers; then at mother, and me. Then he completely surprised, and scared, me with the rough sound that came from his throat. Mother wasted no time rushing to me, pushing me towards the lorry. The soldiers passed the joke all the way round the barricade. In the lorry, we waited for the others to prove they were not of the enemy. The woman on the ground was obscured from view, but I could still hear her wailing. The sky was darkening when we pulled away. We were forced to leave without her.

Mother never stopped chastising me. They shoot people who can't speak their language, she said. As she chastised me, I thought about Monica, who did only what she wanted. I wondered if she would have long enough to say a word when they came for her.

The rest of the journey was not peaceful either. The faces of war leapt up from the tarmac, shimmering illusions in my drowsiness. Armoured trucks, camouflaged with burr, thundered up and down the roads. Planes roared overhead. From time to time a frenzy seized the driver: he would suddenly stop the lorry in the middle of the road and dive for the bushes. Sometimes it took a while to convince him to come out, that we were safe.

'I'm never going to drive again in this madness,' he kept saying.

The taste of madness like the water of potent springs, the laughter of war: that is perhaps why I remember it as a beautiful time. And because in the lorry, with corpses drifting past along the road and soldiers noisy in their jeeps, we were all silent. The weight of our silence was enormous. When we finally arrived I felt like I had seen several lifetimes go past.

Loud cheering and hooting broke out as our lorry swung into the town's garage. People rushed to us from all the silent houses. Children ran with them, cheering and not knowing why. We came down and were thronged by people who wanted to know how the war was doing, how many dead bodies we saw. The driver told them all the stories they wanted to hear.

Mother didn't like the bicycle taxis, which were the only taxis in operation, so she made us walk home. There

were soldiers everywhere. Hysteria blew along the
streets, breathed over the buildings and huts.

When father saw us coming up the street I heard him
shout that the chicken should be caught. It turned out to
be an unruly little chicken with a red cloth tied to its leg,
one that had been bought expensively and saved up
during that time of food shortage. We had been expected
for some time and father was afraid something bad had
happened. They had all grown a little fond of the
chicken. Father opened a bottle of Ogogoro and made
profuse libations to our ancestors, thanking them for
allowing our safe passage home. Father made me bathe
in herbal water, to wash the bad things of the journey off
me. Then the chicken was killed and cooked and served
with Portuguese sardines, boiled cassava, little green
tomatoes and some yam.

And then I started looking out of our window, stirring
as I looked, down our street, past the yellowing leaves of
the guava tree and the orange tree, with its mottled
trunk, that was planted the year I was born, past the
cluster of hibiscus and passion plants, looking at the
house which was really a squat bungalow, where she
lived with her family, ten in all, in one room. And with
a small part of my mind I heard the old ones in the
sitting-room, their voices cracked by the searing alcohol,
as they talked in undertones about the occupation of the
town, about the ones who had died, or gone mad, or the
ones who had joined the army and promised good things
and turned in the heat of battle and fired at their own
men.

When mother came to urge me to sleep, I asked, as
though it were her responsibility:

'Where's Monica?'

'Why are you asking me? Haven't we both just come
from a journey?'

'Where is she?'

Mother sighed.

'How would I know? Before I left she was staying with us. The townspeople pursued them from their house and the family are scattered in the forests. They killed her brother.'

'Which one?'

'Ugo.'

I felt sick.

'So where is she then?'

'What sort of question is that? Nobody in the house knows where Monica is. Sometimes she comes back to the house to eat and then she disappears for several days and then she comes back again. You know how stubborn she is. The day before I came to collect you she went to the market and got into some trouble with a soldier. The soldier nearly shot her. It was your father's good name which saved her.'

I wanted to go out, to find her.

'We are thinking of sending her to the village. The way she is behaving they will kill her before the war is over. You always liked her. When she comes back, talk to her. You will soon be a man, you know.'

Flattered by the last thing she said, for I was only ten, I got up.

As I went out through the door, father said: 'Don't go far-o! There's a curfew. This is not a holiday, you hear?'

At the backyard the other kids said they hadn't seen her all day. I went to the town's market, which sprawled along the length of the main road all the way to the bridge. Couldn't find her. I went round all the empty stalls of the butchers, where she sometimes went to collect offal, which she had a talent for cooking. Couldn't find her. I went to the record shop that overlooked an abattoir of cow and sheep bones. Went to the palm wine bars where she sometimes sold wine to the hungry bachelors and old men of the town: they were now full of soldiers. I went from one rubber plantation to another, walking through tracts of forest sizzling with insects, listening to the rubber pods explode through tangles of branches and crash on the ground. Still couldn't find her.

When I got home father was in a furious temper. Monica stood by the door, her head drooping, staring mulishly at the floor. Father shouted that he didn't want to be responsible for anyone's death, that this was a war, and so on. Father finished shouting at her and she rushed out and went and stood beneath the mango tree, scratching herself, slapping at mosquitoes. It was getting dark. The fragrance of mango fruit was on the wind.

'Monica!' I called.

'Get away!' she screamed at me.

'Where have you been? I've been looking every . . .'

'Get away from here!' she screamed even louder. I went away, up the street. I walked past the post office and came back. She was still leaning against the tree, her eyes hard. I went on into the sitting-room, where I slept at night on a mat on the floor. Later she tapped on the window with a mango branch. I opened the window and she climbed in.

'Let's go out,' she whispered. She saw father's Ogogoro bottle and took a swig of the alcohol.

'Get away!'

'Let's go out,' she said again.

'Where were you today? I searched for you all over town.'

'Look at your big nose,' she said, 'full of pimples.'

'Leave my nose alone.'

She always had such a peppery mouth. She went on abusing me.

'Your head like a bullet,' she said. 'You no tall, you no short, you be like Hausa dagger.'

'What about you? Anyway, where have you been that no one can find you?'

'You're such a fool,' she whispered.

Then she went quiet. She seemed to travel away from her body a little bit and then she came back. All that time I had been telling her about our journey and the soldiers and the lizards. She sort of looked at me with strange eyes and I wanted to draw close to her, to hold her, wrestle with her.

But she said: 'Let's go out.'

'Where?'

'I won't tell you.'

'What about the curfew?'

'What about it?'

'What about the soldiers?'

'What about them?' she asked, taking another swig, the alcohol dripping down her mouth on to her lap. She coughed and her eyes reddened.

'I'm not going. I'm sleepy. They are killing people, you know!'

'So you are afraid of them?'

'No, I'm not.'

'You are a fool.'

She looked me up and down. She pouted her lips. She climbed back out of the window. And I followed.

There was a moon coming over the mango tree.

She went out of the compound and up the street and then turned into another compound. I got there and found a group of kids standing beneath a hedge of hibiscus. Two of them carried great wads of raffia trailings. One of them held a big and ugly mask. Another had little drums surrounding him.

I felt left out.

'Who's building an Egungun?' I asked in as big a voice as I could muster.

'Why do you want to know?' came from, of all people, Monica.

'I want to dance the Egungun. I have not danced it for a long time.'

'Why don't you go and build your own?'

I ignored her and went to the other kids and tried to rough them up a little. None of them said anything. There was a long silence and I listened to the wind moaning underneath the moon. I watched the kids as they went on building the Egungun, sticking raffia trailings to the mask. They strung threads through the corals, which would eventually become bracelets and anklets and make joyous cackles when dancing. The drummer tapped on one of the drums. He got a little carried away. Someone opened a window and shouted at us to stop making noise. One of the boys tried on the mask and shook around. I tried to snatch it from him and Monica said: 'Don't do that. You know you're not allowed to take off an Egungun's mask. You'll die if you do.'

'It's an ugly mask, anyway,' I said, going out from the compound and walking up the street towards the main road. There were a few bicyclists around, furtively looking out for passengers. The moon was big and clear. I heard footsteps. Monica was coming behind me. Two other kids from the group were behind her: ragged companions. I could hear them talking about running away from home to join the army. I suddenly had a vision of my two friends at school, standing in the expanse of fields, surrounded by lizards. I said a prayer for them.

We walked alongside the market. Its arcade of rusted zinc roofing was totally dark underneath: but above it was bright with the moon. The piles of refuse continued all the way past the market.

In the moonlight we could see that there was a roadblock just after the bridge. Mosquitoes were madly whining. Soldiers sat around on metal chairs, smoking intensely in the dark. Their armoured truck, a solitary bulk, covered the road. The other two kids said they were going back, that their parents would be worried about them. I wanted to go back too. I didn't like the way the soldiers smoked their cigarettes. I didn't like the sound of the laughter that came from around the truck.

But Monica was determined to go past them.

The other kids stopped and said they were going to improve on the Egungun. They didn't look too happy about going back. They turned and went sadly alongside the dark and empty market. I looked for Monica and found that she was already over the bridge. I had to run and catch up with her before she got to the soldiers.

They stopped us as we went past.

'Where do you think you are going?'

'Our father sent us a message,' Monica said.

The soldier who had spoken got up from the metal chair. Then he sat down again.

'What message? What message? Is your father mad? Doesn't he know we are fighting a war? Does he think that killing Biafrans is a small thing? Is he mad?'

Monica fidgeted with her toes on the asphalt. The other soldiers smoked stolidly in the dark, taking a mild interest in us. The soldier who had been shouting asked us to move closer. We did. He was a stocky man with an ill-fitting uniform. He had bulging cheeks and a paunch. He looked at Monica in a funny way. He looked at her breasts and then at her neck.

He said: 'Come closer.'

'Who? Me?' I asked.

'Shut up!' he said. Then to Monica: 'I said, *come closer*.'

Monica moved backwards.

The soldier stood up suddenly and his rifle fell from his lap and clattered on the road. I ducked, half-expecting it to fire. He scooped it up angrily and, to Monica, said: 'You be Yamarin?'

Monica stiffened.

'We're from this town,' I said haltingly, in our language.

The soldier looked at me as though I had just stepped in from the darkness.

'Who is your father?'

'The District Commissioner,' I said, lying.

He eyed Monica, stared at her legs. He scratched his nose, fingered his gun, and pulled his sagging military pants all the way up his paunch. He looked as though he was confronted with the biggest temptation of his adult life. Then he touched her. On the shoulder. Monica stepped back, pulled me by my shirt sleeve, urged us to hurry. Soon Monica was in front and her buttocks moved in a manner I hadn't noticed before. We turned and went down the bank of reeds alongside the stream. We sat under a tree and soon a terrible smell came from the water and it stayed a long time and after a while I didn't notice it.

Monica was restless. I had an amazing sense of inevitability. The last time I tried something on Monica she swiped me viciously on the head. Blooming had the effect of making her go around with an exaggerated sense of herself. She always believed she'd marry a prince.

She said: 'I feel like going to war.'

'As what?'

'A soldier. I want to carry a gun. Shoot. Fire.'

'Shut up.'

She was quiet for a moment.

'You know they killed Ugo?'

I nodded. Her eyes were very bright. I had this feeling that she had been changed into something strange: I looked at her face and it seemed to elude me. The moon was in her eyes.

'This is where they dumped his body. It's floated away now.'

She was crying.

'Shoot a few people. Fire. Shoot,' she said. Then she got up and tried to climb the gnarled trunk of the iroko tree. Couldn't do it. She stopped trying to climb and then stood staring at the stream. The soldiers were laughing above the bridge, their boots occasionally crunching the gravel. I went to Monica and she pushed me away. I went to her again and she shoved me away so hard that I fell. I lay down and watched her.

'This is where I've been. All day I sit here and think.'

I went to her and held her round the waist and she didn't do anything. I could smell her armpit, a new smell to me. Above on the bridge, one of the soldiers laughed so hard he had to cough and spit at the end of it.

'Do you see the stream?' she asked me, in a new voice.

'Yes.'

'What do you see?'

'I see the stream with the moonlight on the rubbish.'

'Is that all?'

'Yes.'

'Look. Look. That's where Ugo was. I measured the place with this tree.'

Then something shifted in my eyes. The things on the water suddenly looked different, transformed. The moment I saw them as they were I left her and ran up the bank. The stream was full of corpses that had swollen, huge massive bodies with enormous eyes and bloated cheeks. They were humped along on the top of the water. The bridge was all clogged up underneath with waterweeds and old engines and vegetable waste from the market.

'Monica!'

She was silent. The smell from the stream got terrible again.

'Monica!'

Then she started to laugh. I had never heard that sort of twisted laughter before. After a while I couldn't see her clearly and I called her and she laughed and then I thought it was all the swollen corpses that were laughing.

'Monica! I am going home-o!'

One of the soldiers fired a shot into the air. I rushed down and grabbed Monica. She was shivering. Her mouth poured with saliva, her face was wet. I held her close as we passed the armoured truck. She was jabbering away and I had to cover her mouth with my palm. We didn't look at the soldiers. I could smell their sweat.

When we got home we both came down with a fever.

By Saturday the town had begun to smell. All the time I lay in bed, feverish and weak, the other kids brought me stories of what was happening. They said that at night swollen ghosts with large eyes clanked over the bridge. They said the soldiers had to move from the bridge because the smell of the stream got too strong for them.

I saw very little of Monica. It seemed she recovered faster than I did. When I saw her again she looked very thin and her eyes were mad. There was a lot more talk of sending her to the village. I learnt that in the bungalow behind the hibiscus hedge they were building a mighty Egungun – one that would dwarf even the one with which ja-ja johnny walked over the River Niger, long ago before the world came to be like this. I asked who would ride the Egungun and the others still wouldn't say. On Saturday afternoon I was just strong enough to go and see this new masquerade for myself. The town stank. It was true: the boys had built this wonderful Egungun with a grotesque laughing mask. The mask had been broken – they say Monica's temper was responsible – but it was gummed back together.

In my loudest voice I said: 'I will dance the Egungun.'

They stared at me and then fled, as though they had seen another spirit.

How could it have been a beautiful time when that afternoon the smell got so strong that gas masks and wooden poles had to be distributed to respectable and proven citizens of the town so that they could prod the bodies and clear the rubbish to enable the corpses to flow away beneath the bridge? We saw these respectable citizens marching down our street. They were doctors, civil servants, businessmen, police constables. Their pot-bellies wobbled as they marched. They had the gas masks on. Mother spat when they passed us. The kids in the street jeered at them.

When they had gone I went to the building-place of the Egungun and found that the group was ready to dance along the market and all the way round town. Two small Egunguns warmed up and shook their feet while they waited for the main one. Then we heard a flourish of drums from the backyard and the main Egungun came dancing vigorously towards us. We cheered. Too weak to do anything else, I ended up getting a rope that controlled the main one.

We danced up the street and down the market road. The drumming was strong. The masquerade danced with a wild frenzy, the bracelets and anklets contributing to the rough music. Occasionally the Egungun tore away from my grip and the others blamed me and I had to run and catch the rope and restrain its ferocity. We shouldered bicyclists from the road, danced round old men and women, rattling the marracas made out of Bournvita cans and bird-seeds. When we got to the empty market the spirit of Egunguns entered us. As we danced round the stalls, in the mud of rotting vegetables and meat, we were suddenly confronted by a group of big huge spirits. They were tall, their heads reached the top of the zinc roofing. They had long faces and big eyes. We ran, screaming, and regrouped outside the market. We went towards the bridge.

The Egungun didn't want to cross the bridge. The small ones were dancing over and we were beating our drums across and singing new songs and we turned and found the main Egungun still behind, refusing to come with us. We went back and flogged it and pulled and pushed; but it didn't want to go. The other boys suggested we stone the Egungun. I suggested that we drown it. Then finally the Egungun turned round and we followed, singing ja-ja johnny to the ground, hitting the drums, beating the marracas on our thighs. We danced past the shop of the only tailor in town, whose sign read: TRAINED IN LONDON; and the barber's shed that bore the legend: NO JUSTICE IN THIS WORLD; and past the painter of signboards (who had all sorts of contradictory legends nailed round his shed). We bobbed in front of the houses of the town that were built with the hope that they would, at least, be better than their neighbours. Nobody threw us any coins. None of the grown-ups liked us dancing at that time and they drove us away and abused us. We danced our way back up town again. At the market we saw a confusion of several other Egunguns. We didn't know where they had sprung from. They rattled tin castanets, beat drums, brandished whips.

We clashed with them. We fought and whipped one another under the blazing sun. We toppled stalls and threw stones and spat and cursed, sending a wild clamour through the market. The drummers went completely mad competing amongst themselves. We fought and the commotion increased till some soldiers ran over from the bridge and shouted at us. When we heard the soldiers we took cover behind the fallen stalls. Only our Egungun – an insane laughing mask split in the middle of the face – went on as if nothing had happened. It danced round the stalls, provocatively shaking its buttocks, uttering its possessed language, defying the soldiers.

'Stop dancing! Stop dancing!' one of them thundered. Our Egungun seemed only to derive more frenzy from the order. Then one of the soldiers stepped forward, tore the mask off the Egungun's face, and slapped Monica so hard that I felt the sound. Then suddenly her eyes grew large as a mango and her eyelids kept twitching.

'Speak your language!' the soldier shouted, as her thighs quivered. 'Speak your language!' he screamed, as she urinated down her thighs and shivered in her own puddle. She wailed. Then she jabbered. In her language.

There was a terrible silence. Nobody moved. The soldiers dragged Monica towards the bridge and on to the back of a jeep. When the jeep sped off, raising dust in its rear, there was a burst of agitation and wailing and everybody began to mutter and curse at once and the spirits in the market were talking too, incoherently and in feverish accents. I ran home to tell father what had happened. He rushed out in a very bad temper and I didn't hear what abuse he came out with because when we got to the market a cry of exultation from the men in gas masks told us that the stream had been cleared. The rubbish had gone.

Father rushed on angrily to the army barracks. We passed the bridge and I saw the great swollen bodies as they flowed reluctantly down the narrow stream. I never saw Monica again. The young shall grow.

Converging City

WHEN AGODI WOKE up in the morning it seemed that the spirit was still with him. Sunbeams came through the window and played on his face. The first flash of light he saw when he opened his eyes made him think of Saul's blinding. He remembered that he should pray.

He knelt by the bed in the single room and prayed through his mouth's staleness, but without his usual passion. He felt cheated of an audience. His wife had gone to the market where she sold garri. His two children were at school. When he finished his prayer he made his way over the disorder of empty sacks and blackened cooking utensils and fetched a cup of water from the earthenware pot. He washed out his mouth through the window while thinking about his financial crisis. He spat a mouthful of water down on to the street and the water fell on a girl who had just detached herself from the crowd. The girl stopped and immediately proceeded to abuse him. Her lips were painted red and she wore red earrings. Her high-heeled shoes made her legs look very thin. Agodi mimed an apology, but the girl was unappeased.

'God hammer your head,' she shouted up at him.

'Who? Me?'

'Yes, you, your very wretched self!' she said, relaxing into an impregnable posture of derision. 'It is you I am talking to, you who spits water down at people. You are a goat. You are not a man. You are a shameless fool with nothing better to do but spit water at people. You will die spitting.'

Benevolently, Agodi said: 'Is it because of a small thing like this that you're shouting, eh? If you have so many problems, I will pray for you . . .'

Interrupting, the girl said: 'Pray for your wretched self! I don't blame you. I blame your mother for allowing your father to touch her.'

Agodi was half-way through his invocation on her behalf when he heard the reference to his father. He stammered. Then thunderously he shouted: *The devil block your anus.*

And he tore downstairs after her.

He had rushed down one flight of stairs when he realized that all he had on was a wrapper. He stopped. He started to go back up. But the combination of sunlight on the filthy staircase and the magnitude of her insult aroused in him a peculiar humility. He decided to preach to her; there seemed no telling where a conversion might occur. He ran down the remaining flight of stairs and burst out into the street. Startled by the blasts of music pouring from the record shops, he soon found himself entangled in the hectic crowd.

He looked for the girl and saw her a little way up the road. She made furious insulting signs at him. He ran after her, shouting: 'You, this girl: the word of God is calling you today! I accept the sacrifice of your sinful life. You abuse my father, I pray for your mother. Why are you running? The word of God is calling you and you are running.'

The crowd cleared a path for him. The girl was already in full flight; she ran awkwardly in her high-heels. Agodi raged after her. Voices in the crowd asked if that was his wife fleeing from his insane desires or if she was a prostitute who had infected him with gonorrhoea. Agodi ignored the voices. Anxious to keep the girl in view, he pushed past a man who had been waddling along like a monstrous duck. Agodi's fingers were soon caught in the man's agbada sleeve.

'Are you mad?' the man asked, as he tripped Agodi with a wedged foot. Agodi fell, struggled back up, and found himself confronting a short man whose face was lit up with an expansive, demented smile. The man looked like an abnormally developed midget. He gathered the folds of his agbada on his shoulder and Agodi saw his glistening muscles and the veins bunched along his short arms.

'You want to fight?' the man asked with polite relish. He had incredible face marks. He looked as though he had been reluctantly rescued from a fire. Agodi backed away and looked regretfully at the girl, who was disappearing in the crowd.

'If you don't want to fight, then you must hapologize now.'

Agodi apologized in the name of the Almighty. Playing with his agbada and slowly flexing his muscles, the man said that he found the apology unsatisfactory. Spinning up the interest of the crowd, he said that the god he worshipped accepted only dog-meat as sacrifice. Agodi stammered. With great deliberation, for a few girls had appeared in their midst, the man asked Agodi to repeat his apology. Agodi didn't hear what the man said because he became aware of everyone spitting. He grew conscious of the smell of a rotting body. Sweating and confused, Agodi wondered if the smell came from his antagonist. Then he located the corpse of an up-turned and bloated cow at the side of the road. Exulting flies formed a buzzing black cloud above the swollen body. Agodi had barely recovered from the surprise when the man tapped him twice on the head. Angered by the short man's audacity, Agodi held his fists before him. He hopped and goaded the man and at the same time made pleading insinuations about the fires of hell, the agony of sinners. The man found his cue. He made a strange noise and held Agodi in a curious grip and then tossed him into the air. When Agodi landed it was with a squelchy explosion as he scattered the flies and was immediately covered in a burst of foul-smelling liquids. Beyond the wild sounds, and the jubilant flies, he saw the world pointing at him. He pulled himself out, using the horn as lever. When he had extricated himself from the belly of the cow he found his wrapper irredeemably soaked.

The city followed him as he shambled back to the house. A contingent of flies followed him as well. The children jeered at him. The man who had hurled him into shame was meanwhile busily distributing his business cards. His gestures were magnanimous and he had a disconcerting smile for everyone. His card read: COACH IN ACTION. PROFESSIONAL EX-WRESTLER. I OFFER PROTECTION OF PROPERTY, PETROL STATIONS, COMPOUNDS AND STREETS. AVAILABLE FOR ALL OPERATIONS. TRAINED ROUND THE WORLD. His name was Ajasco Atlas.

When he finished distributing the cards he shook hands with several people. He told them that he had just come from India. They were impressed. The girls had gathered round him. He was seen leaving with them.

Agodi hid himself in the bathroom. He thought how every single person in the world had witnessed his shame. The news would certainly reach the Church of

Eternal Hope. He was due to get a small loan from the church. He had been with them, as a faithful servant and crusader, for five years now. The Head Minister had explained how a church should also be a bank that keeps its members safe. The funds were controlled by a strict inner circle of elders. They gave out loans only in times of absolute need and on the strength of conduct glorifying the church. Agodi thought about all this while he washed the suppurating liquids from his body. Out of the corner of his eye, he saw a millipede crawling along the rotted plank wall. He saw three earthworms stretching their way through the wet sand that flowed out with the water. He blew his nose and his snot landed on the back of the millipede. He blamed himself severely for not having turned the other cheek; at the same time he knew that he wouldn't be alive now if he had. The ways of the world, he thought, were wickedly unjust. He dried himself and went back upstairs.

Agodi anointed himself with coconut oil. Then he lit three candles and a stick of incense and prayed for thirty minutes. The prayer consisted of one long sentence, breathlessly articulated. Wrestling with the demons of language, he asked for peace and prosperity, he begged that the news of his disgrace should not reach the church, and he wished havoc on all his enemies.

When he finished with his prayer he felt sufficiently charged. He felt that he could now possess the day. He was almost sure that the city would concede what the fervour of his prayer had sanctioned. His body ached all over. He got dressed. He wore a thread-loose French suit which conferred on him a hint of suffering dignity.

He went downstairs to his little shop, which was situated in front of the house. It was a slanted wooden shed with rusted zinc roofing. It was painted blue and it had a padlock. He sold items of clothing: shirts, trousers,

Italian shoes and fabrics, sunshades and wigs. Most of the goods had been smuggled into the country with the collaboration of officials at the docks. His signboard read: J. J. AGODI AND SONS. GENERAL CONTRACTORS. IMPORTING AND EXPORTING. TRY US FOR SIZE. A TRIAL WILL CONVICT YOU. When Agodi went in he repossessed the spirit of the shed in prayer. It was stuffy inside. The available space had been shrunken with wooden chairs and unsold goods. Old newspapers, which he had never read, were in disarray about the floor. He didn't notice the letter that had been sent to him. He tried to open the window, but found that it had got stuck. He tried to force it open, but a splinter caught in his flesh. He banged his fist against the window, half-expecting the wooden frame to disintegrate. Nothing happened. He tried the window again and it opened without fuss.

He compiled his accounts for the week. He had made very little money. No one showed much interest in his goods. Enquiries were few, buyers were even fewer. He hoped that the small consignment at the wharf would change all that. He played around with his accounts as though, by applying some mathematical trick, he could effect a multiplication. His armpits became wet. The month's rent was overdue. There was a hunger in his calculations that made him aware of the city outside the shed. He heard the scrapings of a rat. A chafer fanned past his face. A lizard scuttled half-way up the wall. Agodi caught the lizard in a gaze and was surprised that it stared back at him. He looked for an object and was lost in the multiplicity of things which could come in handy. The lizard nodded. Agodi surreptitiously eased off a shoe, threw it, and missed by several feet. The lizard nodded. Agodi grabbed a handful of newspapers and before he threw them he discovered that the lizard had gone. Only its tail writhed on the floor.

He thought about his money problems. He looked at his watch. It had stopped. He shook it and it started ticking again. He gave it an hour. He put his shoe back on. It was time for him to go out into the city.

When he stood up he saw the letter on the floor. It was addressed to the owner of the shed. He opened it and the letter read: 'To the owners of dis shop, We are coming to rub you tonite. If you like call the police. Anytime is good for us.'

Agodi read the letter three times. He creaked his neck and twisted his head. There had always been stories of people receiving letters like this. He could not remember one person who was finally robbed. If thieves are going to pay you a visit, he thought, they don't write you a letter first. But he started to pray. His voice, quivering, turned into a complaint. And the sight of the lizard's tail made him see the city beyond: he saw people lying at street corners, scratching themselves; he saw the youths who grow angrier and then sooner or later turn to armed robbery; he saw those who are executed at the beach; and he saw the children who put a piece of wood into their mouths and die four days later, poisoned by their own innocent hunger. It all came to him in the form of shapeless waves of dizziness. He believed he had just witnessed a revelation. Again he thought of Saul. The real trouble was that he had not yet eaten. He swayed with a minor fit of vertigo. He surmounted the shapes by rallying the powers of the prophets, the Head Minister of his church, and Jesu Christi.

At that moment he might have collapsed if someone hadn't pushed open the door. Saved by the prospect of business and the immediate resolve to charge more than normal, Agodi was surprised that the man who had come in didn't have on a pair of trousers; and his underpants were in very bad condition. The man was very thin and his face was angular. His hair looked as if it had never been intended to be combed. He was so wretched that Agodi screamed. Then he dived for a spanner beneath the table. The man stood staring. When Agodi flung the spanner, the man tore out of the shed. Agodi pursued him.

The man fled across the street. He ran, blindly flailing out against the heat and the noise and the dust. He crossed the full width of the street without being hit by a vehicle. He stopped. Puzzled, he ran back. He paused in the middle of the street and looked both ways. He saw nothing, except for an old woman cycling towards him. When he saw that there were no vehicles along one of the busiest streets in the world he laughed. He also laughed at Agodi, who had rushed out of the shed, brandishing the spanner, shouting that he had single-handedly routed the thieves of the city.

The man in the street revelled in his safety. He marvelled. He rolled over on his back. Cars and buses swerved round him. Drivers abused him. Motorcyclists missed him by the narrowest of inches. Then an intractable traffic jam resulted. Streets and main roads were blocked. Cars and lorries stood bumper to bumper. The whole traffic jam soon resembled a long and obscenely metallic millipede.

The Head of State was being driven home after a hectic morning at a trade conference, when his escorts found themselves trapped in the traffic jam. The soldiers and mobile policemen thrashed out in every direction. They kicked the metalwork of cars, pounced on lorry drivers, and beat up people who seemed to be obstructing the traffic in any visible or invisible way. The heat was a tonic and the official escorts were completely in their element.

But the Head of State was furious. He felt that the traffic jam was a particularly perverse way for his people to show how much they wanted him out of office. When he stared at the congestion all around him he experienced a sudden panic. He phoned through to Intelligence and demanded an immediate unwinding of the traffic jam by any means possible. When he looked up he saw, in the shape of an earthworm moving across the tinted window, the shadow of his executioner. Watching the earthworm out of the corner of his eye, he scribbled down notes about a new decree for the swift reduction of traffic jams.

Suddenly a shot was fired, which cracked the glass, and missed his head. He fell forward, a trained, if flaccid, soldier. He heard a further volley of shots. He had heard them every night for the past five years. He clutched the notes. He waited. He heard nothing. Minutes later he was told that he was out of danger. The plotters had been killed. Then the traffic jam eased, and vehicles started to move.

The Head of State decided to change his country. He wrote down a list of decrees to be discussed as soon as possible with the Supreme Military Council. He wrote down a very long list and soon ran out of paper. As the official vehicle eased back fully into motion, the Head of State looked over his jottings. Listening to the wailing sirens, he decided that the decrees were impractical and designed only to create martyrs. He had to think of his own safety as well as the entangled safety of his embezzlements. He knew that there would be even more attempts on his life if one word got out of his new efforts to clean up the stables. For the first time, he realized that he didn't really rule the country. He had no idea who did. Hot air blew at him from the shattered window and he tore up the notes with more energy than was necessary. When his motorcade turned into his barracks, when he saw the clean stretch of tree-lined road ahead,

he immediately decided that the civilians had better
return. Let them carry the cross of the country. He was
going where the earthworms go.

The man in the street, who had started the traffic jam in
the first place, attempted to get up. He was starving. He
staggered and fell. People rushed over and picked him
up. They dumped him at the side of the street. They
asked him what was wrong with him and he said:
sardines and Fanta. They left him in a hurry.

The man in the street lay there all through the day. He
watched the dust rise. He watched the air saturate with
smoke and he heard the desperate music that rode over
the area. He saw arguments that led to fights. He saw the
rich and how they created the poor. He saw the mice and
how they fed on the poor. It amused him. He heard those
with invisibly splayed feet, who were stalked all day and
all night. He heard those that did the stalking. They were
legion. He also heard Agodi start his Vespa and saw him
ride out into the city. When Agodi was gone, the man in
the street found the serenity to sleep. He nodded in his
dreams.

As Agodi rode into the city he saw people at bus stops
fighting to get on the buses: and he was glad that he had
maintained his Vespa. At the Iddo garage he saw two
women wrestling. They tore at one another's clothes till
they were both nearly naked. Agodi parked. Soon many
people gathered to watch the staged fight. Three soldiers
circled the barricade beside the road. A man clambered
on top of a trailer and delivered himself of a lengthy
speech, which few people heard, on why destruction
must fall on soldiers, thieves and prostitutes. He de-
nounced the regime. He said fire was coming; and before
he finished, one of the women was thrown. Suddenly

the soldiers found that their money and identity cards had been stolen. They went berserk and cracked their new horsewhips on the gathered crowd. Agodi rejoiced that he was a man of God. And rode on.

Being a man of God didn't help him at the wharf. He had to sit in a hot outshed and wait for his contact man. He waited till he began to feel dizzy with the heat. Then he went out and got himself a snack and a soft drink. When he came back he found that his contact man had been impatiently waiting for him. The contact man told Agodi straightaway that his smuggled goods had been seized.

He said: 'My friend, the Inspector is very angry with what you offered. He says it's a mere pittance. Birdshit.'

Agodi stammered.

The contact man said: 'That's the way things go.'

Agodi knew what he had to do. But he tried conversion first. He told the contact man about the wonders of God; about how a man might be one thing one day, and the exact opposite the next. Agodi preached till sweat poured into his mouth.

The contact man was neither moved nor intimidated by God's reversals. He said: 'Save your saliva, my friend. Money na hand, back na ground.'

Agodi calculated that he could spare another fifty naira. He offered. The contact man took it as an insult. He walked away slowly. Agodi swallowed.

The man said: 'They will just burn your things for nothing. You can't be serious. If you are serious you will know what to say. You have the money, my friend.'

Agodi fought his tears. He pleaded. The man ignored him. Then Agodi tried to abase himself to the point where, out of shame and human feeling, the contact man just might relent. He listed his problems.

But the contact man's face was so unforgivingly impassive it might have been made of stone. He said:

'You are wasting my time. I didn't come here to listen to your problems. I have my own wahala, you hear? Either you want to collect or you don't want to collect. Which one you dey, eh? Tell me, make I hear.'

Agodi made promises. The man yawned. Agodi asked for a day's grace. The contact man chewed on the idea for almost a day before he finally consented. Agodi climbed on his Vespa, feeling that he had salvaged something from a really desperate situation.

He needed money. The church was completely out of it. He had not only slackened in attendance, but there was also the business of the cow. His wife was also out of it. He owed her too much money already. Every night, when she returned from the market, she looked more burnt and punished. Her eyes were now permanently red from the dust and pepper of the market. Her cheekbones stood out in relief and her spirit had hardened. She was definitely out of it. Besides, she was paying for the children's school uniforms.

Agodi rode around the city casting for ways of getting money to save his goods. He visited friends and relatives in their offices and in their homes. They were not particularly pleased to see him. They gave him food, but they had no money to lend him. He owed most of them enough as it was. Night fell and Agodi rode back home.

The man in the street had seen a whole day pass and had learnt nothing. He had settled himself near a gutter. He covered himself with unread newspapers. He lay down, as if dead, though he jerked in delirium now and again. He watched Ajasco Atlas, who had gone past a few times, shouting about his feats in India. Ajasco Atlas had been intimidating people into accepting his business cards. He told everyone that he was an ex-world champion. He told them that he was a businessman as well. All-weather. He said he participated in the capture of two cities during the war and that he had done business with even the Head of State. All day he had warned people that if they were robbed it was entirely their own fault. He considered that he had done his best in offering cheap protection. Ajasco Atlas had, in fact, opened a small office along the street and was seen doing the most astonishing exercises in public.

The man in the street also watched the shed of J. J. Agodi with special zeal. He was the only person who saw the road move. He saw the henchmen of Ajasco Atlas move. Then he saw the shed as it moved gently. He saw it raised high as if lifted by a mighty and erratic hand. Then the shed disappeared into the darkness of the street.

Agodi rode into the compound and meticulously locked the Vespa. He thought about doing some very serious calculations. One hundred naira. The birds of the air feed, he thought. He had arrived at the conclusion that he would have to double his prices. He looked for his shed and he could not find it. The birds of the naira. He wandered around the compound, he went to the backyard. And still he couldn't find his shed. Saul's blindness. He called to his compound people, he called to the great wide world to come and see the extent of his suffering. Saul's one hundred naira. The world came and stared at the empty space where a battered little shed had once stood. They saw nothing except for the carcase of a lizard. They stared at the lizard and stared at Agodi. One by one they left.

Agodi sat out all night watching the space where the shed had been. He waited for his act of repossession. He abused the city. He grew hoarse. He gathered his wife and two children together. His wife was exhausted to the point of sleepwalking. He asked them to pray for the return of the shed. He started to cry and his wife severely rebuked him. The children cried and she joined them.

The man in the street, who nodded in his dreams, learned something. A very small thing. He learned where the earthworms go.

Agodi stayed up all night staring at the dead lizard. When dawn broke he fetched some holy water and poured the whole bottle on the lizard. Nothing happened. Agodi prayed and prayed. He felt the spirit leaving him. Then he called for kerosene and fire.

A week later Agodi rebuilt the shed. It did not have its former glory. He did not use it. Nobody wanted to rent it either. His consignment was sold off at the wharf. Then one morning his wife took the children and fled home to her village.

Agodi suddenly disappeared. Nobody saw him for a month. When Agodi reappeared he was seen wearing a purple-and-yellow robe. He had grown a reddish beard and his hair was in tiny braids. He announced that in the forests of the city he had achieved blindness and had seen God. He declared that he was now a true prophet. God and money, he said, were inseparable. He founded a new church and had several business cards printed. His new signboards sprang up along the busy street. Ajasco Atlas was sometimes seen around the premises. Everyone has problems.

While things improved, Agodi became aware of the man in the street, who had obsessively taken to watching him. Sometimes Agodi was sure that the man was making curious faces at him from across the street. And sometimes Agodi remembered the lizard that he had burned on that terrible morning. It had simply turned into air.

Disparities

I DO NOT know what season it is. It might be spring, summer or winter, for all anyone cares. Autumn always misses me for some reason. It probably is winter. It always seems to be winter in this damn poxy place. When the sun is up and people make a nuisance of themselves, revealing flaccid and shapeless bodies, I am always aware of a chill in my marrow. My fingers tremble. My toes squash together. And my teeth chatter. That is the worst; there is more. And when the severity of the grey weather returns, when the seasons run into one another, and when advertisements everywhere irritate the eye and spirit – depicting vivid roses, family togetherness and laughter mouth-deep – I cannot help feeling that civilizations are based on an uneasy yoking of lies; and that is precisely when the sight of flowers and pubs and massive white houses and people depresses me most; when, in fact, I am most nauseated. Then I have constant fits of puking, nervous tremulation and withdrawal symptoms so merciless that I cannot separate the world from the sharp exultant pangs in my chest. My resistance is low. The only season I know from this side of the battering days is starvation. I know it is warm when I have filled my stomach with a tin of baked beans; it is tepid when I must have had a piece of toast; and it is cold when I have bloated my stomach on a pint of milk some idiot left standing on a doorstep. When an individual learns to cope with the absurdity of seasons without changing trivial externalities – *then*, in my estimation, *they* have acquired the most vital trappings of culture. All else is just overlaid loneliness and desperation and group brutality.

The trouble is I lived in a house for a few days. My first house. It was all peaceful and full of dogshit and totally decrepit. The walls had been broken down, cushions torn, the windows fitted with gashed rubbish-bin linings. It was a lovely place; I had never before found such serenity. To have a house, that is the end of the journey of our solitude.

Then, of all the horrible things that can happen to disrupt such a discovery – a bunch of undergraduates moved in upstairs. They made a hell of a lot of noise, had long drinking and smoking parties, talked about books and 1940s clothes and turbans and dope from exotic places and the Vice-Chancellor. They brought with them a large tape-recorder and played reggae and heavy metal music. Then they brought in mattresses, pillows, food, lampshades, silk screens and large lurid posters and *books*. Imagine my revulsion. They talked about Marx and Lévi-Strauss and Sartre and now and then one of the girls would say how easy it was to appreciate those *bastards* (she said this laughingly) when one is stoned.

That was it. Definitely. It was enough that one had to bear oneself in a single frame, but to add to that a bunch of undergraduates who were playing holiday games with broken and empty houses was more than any person could stand without going berserk. A genocidal mood gripped me. I got my bundle together and stormed upstairs. The house was in a far worse state of devastation than I imagined. The banisters had all been knocked down and attempts had been made to wreck the stairs. The rooms were bad. I banged around up into the higher reaches of the house and eventually found the students.

The door to their room had been broken down. There were about six of them. Group desolation. Indeed, they were all variations of a type: their hair dyed red or blue or purple; they wore tight-fitting trousers, the girls wore desperate short dresses, and their eyelids were painted with iridescent sheen. I found it impossible to see one for the other; they seemed so interchangeable. The room had been cleared up, it was almost – a *room*. There were mirrors all over the place and their interchangeability, reflecting back and forth, compounded my confusion. When I banged in they were lying down, coupled, women to women, men to men, women to men. They jerked their heads, responding awkwardly to the reggae music.

For a long moment words escaped me. One of them said something about going home and returning shortly; another replied, saying that this was a good 'scene' and forget home and 'check it out, yeh.' Another said: 'Yeh, pass the joint' – and for some group reason they all *laughed*. Two things happened inside me: I was angry; and I instantly became aware of a low point in my season. I didn't want to eat or anything like that; I was simply possessed with the desire to retch. Instead, I kicked one of their mirrors. They *laughed*. One of them said: 'Hey, man, are you the *landlord*?' And another said: 'Pass the joint.' And another: 'Join the party.' And another one (laughingly): 'I tell you, right: *we are landlords.*' The voices merged and became cluttered: 'We are Communists. Anarcho-Communists.' My toes felt squashed. '*Get it, right: we are Comfemists.*' My throat began a curious process of strangling me and my head grew livid with twitches. 'WE ARE WHITE. BUT WE ARE FUCKTOGETHERNESS, RIGHT.' There was a diminutive black girl with them. She was cradled by a white girl with a pinched face and elaborate gestures. They were giggling. The music stopped. The girl with the pinched face stood up: 'WE STAND FOR FREEDOM.' I turned around, tripped over some stupid fitting and fumbled my way down the beautiful death trap that was the stairs. When I came out into the street I could still hear them laughing.

Well. So. I was yet again unhoused. Landlords have the queerest ways. Anyway. That was that. And who denies that the system (monster invisible) has the capacity to absorb all its blighted offshoots? And so I took to the streets. The long, endless streets. Plane trees growing from cement. I walked and walked and I inspected the houses as I went along. Houses. I avoided taking in the eye-sores that were human beings and stuck my gaze to the pavement in front of me. This was highly rewarding for I was entertained with the shapes of dogshit. This is the height of civilization. This is what to look out for when everything else seems a nightmare. Following these patterns, and where they seemed to lead, I came to a park.

The park was all right, as parks in this place go. All the usual greenery and undulations and grey statues and rundown cafés and playgrounds. And, of course, there were people. I saw old men and women with dogs. Children playing about in all the sorts of games in which they are for ever trapped as children. They ran about, shouted, cried, called names, laughed, were sweet; they formed little groups and kept the brutality intact; they pretended they were adults, calling the different names of animals and birds and flowers. The older people were no different: they trundled around, looked wistfully at the sky, pretended to enjoy their isolation, called to their dogs, looked on fondly and complacently when their dogs urinated: they smiled at the children, sat stiffly on benches. When the children's football rolled towards them they sometimes kicked it back with a crotchety grace. I saw the young couples nestled together near a tree or in the open fields; they, too, looked complacent – the whole of nature as a lover's dream. They laughed, nice little laughs without any depth and without any pain. Insipid love; cultured laughter. Or they threw balls at one another, stiffly mimicking the children; or they walked slowly along, hair fingered by the wind, their faces pale pink on blue–white. They, too, must enjoy their isolation.

So I followed my compass. Away from the wreckful siege. It pointed north, to the furthest part where there were no landscaped undulations and no lovers and no children of any sort; where only nobbled and ugly trees consorted and where the earth was slashed in the beginnings of some building project recently liberated from red-tape. I first of all eased myself comfortably on one of these trees and then I searched for an area of unattractive grass. Not far from where I was going to sit there was a bird. Maggots crawled out of its beak. I stared at it for a while, all sorts of temptations going through my mind. It was upturned in a grotesque enchantment and for a while I experienced a cluttered remembrance of all those fairy-tales that were bludgeoned into us when young. The memories irritated me. I spat, generously, and then I lay down. There seemed no distance between me and the sky. I hate skies. They seemed to me a sentimental creation. Skies are something else that has been bludgeoned into us. They are everywhere: in adverts, on windowpanes, reflected in patches of dog piss. Hardly a conversation takes place without someone mentioning the sky: hardly you open a novel without the author attempting some sort of description. Honestly. Skies are quite boring. Anyway. I entertained the thought, and I am ashamed of it, and my shame is my business, of how it would be like to be able to leave this body and become part of the sky. The relentless visitations! The upending of myths and the tremendous reversals and the creating of new myths to enable people to become complacent again!

I was about to explore the true foulness of the fantasy when, of all visitations, a bunch of children led by a schoolteacher went past. If they had just tramped past and gone on, and on, it would have been fine. But no. Every sweet solitude had to be destroyed. And they lingered. The teacher told them the names of trees (elm, plane, horsechestnut, etc.), asked them the names of the cloud formations, told them not to fight, asked them to pay attention, and so on. If it had been just a little educational trip it would have been fine. Horrors – the children began to prowl around. They brought back mushrooms, worms skewered on twigs, butterflies cupped in hands; they had a *picnic*. Then at one point the most annoying thing happened: they saw *the enchanted bird*. If there is anything more annoying than the self-conscious giggles of lovers it is the sound of inquisitive children. This is what happened. Three of the kids were running about, chasing one another. They saw me and stopped. They looked at me and looked at each other and then they laughed. They whispered among themselves. Their interest soon vanished. They had seen the bird.

'What is it?'

'It's a bird.'

They stood around the bird. One of them kicked it over and ran away. The others ran with her. They soon came back.

'What is it?'

'It's a dead pigeon.'

'It's a dead pigeon – ooooooh.'

They ran away again and came back.

'What is it?'

'I thought it was a dead duck.'

'A dead duck!'

'It's a *dead pigeon*. Can't you see?'

They poked at the bird again. One of them lifted it up delicately with the tip of her fingers as though it were the most diseased thing imaginable. Then she dropped it.

'Uuuuuuhhhh. It's got maggots all over it.'

They regarded the bird for a moment. There was a morbid fascination in their eyes. I had seen adult mutations of that look several times. It is a look that is perched between the power for terror and the possibility of inflicting that terror. I have seen it highly concentrated, and hidden, when a policeman regards me at night, a moment before he grabs me by the collar and shoves me out of the Tube station where he knows I have to spend the night. I have seen it frustrated and sly when I encounter bands of youths. I have seen it in the men when they think I am more than eyeing their women. And when I saw it then in the eyes of those children I could not restrain myself from yelling. They looked at me. Shocked. I looked at them.

Their teacher, eyeing me with metallic severity, said: 'Jane, leave the bird alone. Come on, come along, girls.'

The girls regarded me with utmost suspicion. They stared at me and stared at the bird. I think they must have ascertained the most intriguing relationship between me and that bird. Fear trembled in their eyes. Fear and eternal curiosity. They waited for one of them to make the first movement. One of them did and the next minute they all fled. I watched them. The teacher moved them on. They talked among themselves and kept looking back at me. Maybe they expected me to turn into a huge black bird and take off into the air.

Anyway, I tried to recover my reverie about some sort of room in the sky where lies and illusions and self-deceptions are made naked; and where humanity can recover its very basic sense of terror and compassion. But nothing is allowed me. A dog came towards me from across the fields. It stopped at the tree where I had earlier on eased myself; it raised a hind leg and urinated. Then it too saw me. Sniffed me out. Barked and barked; and then it discovered the bird. It sniffed the bird, carried it off in its mouth, and brought it back again. The dog's owner, an old man with an absurd sense of self-dignity, trundled past me, saw me, but, thanks to decorum, pretended not to see me.

He stopped, whistled, and said as if to a child: 'Come on, Jimmy.' The dog raced off, and the old man followed. Dogs and their owners always make such a pair. That, again, was that. I got up, made my way through the park and hugged the streets again.

It really does pay to avoid the sight of human beings. I had a windfall; I found a pound note. There it was wet and stuck to the ground among the leaves that had fallen from the plane trees. Plane trees grow from cement. That was that. And it called for a celebration of another minor season. I decided to make my way to a favourite pub in town. When I arrived, pushing aggressively through the door, the barman instantly recognized me and that morbid fascination leapt into his eyes. He licked his lips. He had a bullying face with a wild growth of beard. He was tall. He had that angry and grumpy air of one who had kicked himself out of a rebellious and idealistic generation. I suspected that running the pub was for him an act of masochistically gutting the dreams that had abandoned him. The pub stank thoroughly. It had for its clientele the very cream of leftovers, kicked-outs, eternal trendies, hoboes, weirdos, addicts and pedlars. The foulest exhalations of humanity were nowhere so pungent. The pub and its depressing decor, having soaked in the infinitely varied stinks of its customers, recycled its pollutions free of charge with the drinks. And this is precisely what the pub celebrates. I didn't mind: I had been entangled in enough fights and had uttered enough that was blasphemous to enable me to buy drinks on credit. After all, having a credit is one of the finer things of life.

So the barman watched me. His face twitched. He moved towards me: 'What will it be? Paying up? Or more credit?'

Before I could make up my mind, an old man rushed at me. The wheels grind: and one has to take the grindings as they come. The old man offered to buy me a drink. We had an unstated pact that had been going on for weeks. Whenever I came in he would rush to buy me a drink and then I was supposed to listen to the accumulation of his problems. He told me everything. He told me about how he had hated going to the war. He told me of his first wife, who had made several attempts to kill him; and his second wife, who didn't like sex; and how he gave up wives and discovered prostitutes. He told about his overdrafts, how he contracted VD, his suicide attempts, his varicose veins and how they throbbed and about the cat he bought and was forced to kill one wintry night. It was the way it purred, he said, the way it shivered. He simply inundated me with the grimiest details of his condition. I didn't mind; I had my drinks paid for; and besides, his account of his own suffering had a bracing effect on me. Whenever I saw him I knew that my dose of participation in humanity was assured. Then I could go away, search for a place for the night, and dream about varicose veins and strangled kittens.

He was holding a newspaper. He trembled as if in the grip of a curious sexual fever. His fingers twitched. The barman looked on, his mouth twisted in a peculiar dream of sadism. I ordered two drinks: a half for the old man and a pint for me. The barman licked his lips. The old man stuttered and brought out his crinkled wallet. I fingered my windfall; I laughed. Someone put a coin into the jukebox and plunged that human cesspit into perfect unmelodious gloom. The barman plonked the drinks on the counter, and scowled. I plonked my windfall on the counter, hugged the drinks, and edged the old man into one of the grimy seats.

I tasted my drink and then took a mouthful. The old man smiled. He put his newspaper down on the table and then struggled with his pocket. He was always doing things like that. Grey with decrepit mystery, he brought out a packet of razorblades from the side pocket of his coat.

'I am going to have a shave,' he said.

'Here?'

'No. Later.'

I drank some more. The bar filled up, became crowded, and all the groups that fought for supremacy made their loud noises in the dull lights of the pub. He drank as well. He looked around, from one group to the next, from one spaced-out hippy to another hash-pedlar. He was uncertain. He struggled with his pockets again and brought out a handkerchief. It was stained beyond description.

'You should be a magician,' I said.

He smiled, but his face made it into a mask of anguish. That bilious face! He coughed, looked at me, coughed again. He scraped his throat with the cough, out flew his phlegm. The phlegm – thick, green and sludgy – was trapped between his mouth and the handkerchief. Then it dribbled down his chin. He rescued it with the handkerchief. I could see how the handkerchief got its colour. He smiled again, a perfect mask. He was not satisfied: with another deep-grinding cough he dragged up more phlegm; the same thing happened. I caught myself watching. I could no longer taste my drink; everything soon seemed to be composed of the old man's phlegm. Then he began to talk. Uncertain. He did not know if the pact was still operative; he rambled. He told me of the foxes he saw along the desolate railway tracks at night. He told me of the old woman who had died downstairs. At some point when my disgust had begun to turn upon itself, I told him to stop.

'What's the matter?'

That bilious face!

'I want you to listen to me.'

He nodded. Then without knowing why I began to talk. That's how we do it sometimes. We talk ourselves into the inescapable heart of our predicament. I told him about the number of times I had been beaten up outside Tube stations at night. I told him where I had to sleep, unmentionable places that leave a dampness in the soul. I told him how I wander around the city inspecting the houses with only a tubful of yoghurt in my stomach. I am on hunger-strike, I said. I can't strike and I'm hungry. When I had a fever, only the streets saw me through it. I just went on and on till I got so confused in the heart of what I was saying that all I wanted to do was fall asleep. I was tired; I had drained myself; I stopped. When I looked up, the old man was crying. He sobbed and puckered his lips and scratched his hands. I was irritated. I picked up the newspaper and read the story of a Nigerian who had left a quarter of a million pounds in the

back of a taxi-cab. The old man still wept and kicked on
the seat. Everyone looked at us; they didn't really care; it
was the common run of the place. The old man suddenly
stopped crying. He picked up the packet of razorblades
and made for the toilet. It occurred to me, as he stumbled
against the table and spilled some of our drink, that I
needed razorblades. I followed him and after a scuffle
disarmed the decrepit magician of the packet. He went
back to his chair and I got fed up with the whole farce. I
felt dizzy. I recognized the dizziness: it was the mark of a
low season. When it first happened to me I thought it
was an early sign that I was going mad. Then I learned
that all I really needed was a pint of some idiot's milk and
a can of baked beans.

I got up; I told the old man to have my drink and asked
him for some cigarettes. He threw his well-fingered
packet at me. I went out, avoiding the bullying glance
of the barman, glad to be rid of that insistent sound of
weeping, which is a mark of when people have lost a
temporary haven; and glad also to be rid of that whole
bunch of depressives and trendies who mistake the fact
of their lostness for the attraction of the outsider's
confusion.

As I walked down the darkened streets and inspected
the curtained windows of the houses, I found that I
had discovered something. I had found, in that sweet-
tempered solitude of the streets, a huge and wonderfully
small room in the sky that is composed of ten thousand
taxi-cabs and pasted over with the quarter of a million
pounds that belonged to a Nigerian. And in this discovery I dreamed of several silk-yards of myths and
realities and enchantments with which to remake the
cracked music of all wretched people.

Yes, I dreamed. I had discovered, for example, that
there had been a mistake. Everyone had been fooled: I

had perpetrated a hoax. Nobody knew it but: I WAS THE
TAXI-CAB DRIVER. What a shock it was, coming to myself.
Tramping down the grey streets, inspecting the houses,
I followed myself, haunted by the desires in that hoax.
This is how it happened, not too long ago. I was a
taxi-cab driver, cruising along. This man in a brown suit
flagged me. He had a briefcase. The first thought that
crossed my mind was that he was a Nigerian. Rich
Nigerian. I had picked up several of them before. I
stopped and he climbed in. I looked at him in the mirror.
He looked respectable and had an air of charismatic
indifference. Politician or businessman. He told me
where to drop him and before we got there he decided to
stop off at Marks & Spencer. He stayed there a long time.
He was probably buying up the entire establishment. I
had picked up a few of them and had been pretty
shocked at the number of stereos, videos and boxes of
cereal that they took back home. I waited for the man. Let
it be known that I waited. Then I took one look at the
briefcase and drove away angrily. When I discovered the
quarter of a million pounds in it, the first thing I did was
to dump the cab. I caught a plane to America, bummed
around for a while, came back, and changed my colour.
It seemed to me a simple matter. People have been
executed for much less than leaving a quarter of a million
pounds in a starving man's cab. People, in fact, should
be hanged for carrying that kind of money around. What
more could I do to help the starving, the miserable, the
drought-ridden bastards of this world than to drive off
with such money? That, however, is as far as my solution
got. When I came back, and changed my colour, and saw
all those stupid television news stories of the anguished
Nigerian and the reward he was offering, I simply
laughed my head off. I lugged the briefcase with me
wherever I went. One day I found myself on a bridge

over the Thames. Somehow I trapped myself into one of those moods when you think the whole ineluctable mystery of life is caught in the river's reflections. I saw this white boy on the water flowing beneath the bridge. There was a group of people on the shore; they were shouting. Perfect fool that I was – I allowed a feeling of chivalry to come over me: I jumped into the river. When I splashed into the water I suddenly realized that the briefcase had gone. The boy was nowhere in sight. I swam around and soon saw a body floating, its head beneath the water. I swam after it and several confused thrashings later, the water surging into my mouth, I brought him ashore. The boy was dead and already bloated. The people who were clamouring on the shore, I discovered, had nothing whatever to do with the body. Then I remembered the briefcase. Hungry, wet, haunted by the faces of the anguished Nigerian, I shouted: 'There is a quarter of a million pounds floating on the river.' Before I could dive back in to rescue the briefcase, the inevitable happened. The Thames soon swarmed with a quarter of a million pirates, rogues and hassled people who had long since had enough. They bobbed and kicked, a riot on the waters, for a leather briefcase that would open up a feverish haven of dreams and close up, for ever, the embattled roomful of desires. The police got into it and I slipped away, angry and frustrated and cheated of myself. I hope that they never recovered the money.

That was a dream that drowned.

What a shock it was, coming to myself, when plane trees grow from cement and when the seasons of the streets yielded a dream of wonder. I found a house. I had always wanted to own a house. I inspected it. Bats flew out of the windows. I went up the creaking stairs and peeked around the eerie rooms. There was excreta all over the place, but that was of no serious consequence. I lit a match and found one of the rooms more tolerable than the others. I sat down and took in the smells of rubble and suicides and the decaying of human structures. I looked outside the window and found that it was morning.

Incidents at the Shrine

A NDERSON HAD BEEN waiting for something to fall on him. His anxiety was such that for the first time in several years he went late to work. It was just his luck that the Head of Department had chosen that day for an impromptu inspection. When he got to the museum he saw that his metal chair had been removed from its customary place. The little stool on which he rested his feet after running endless errands was also gone. His official messenger's uniform had been taken off the hook. He went to the main office and was told by one of the clerks that he had been sacked, and that the supervisor was not available. Anderson started to protest, but the clerk got up and pushed him out of the office.

He went aimlessly down the corridors of the Department of Antiquities. He stumbled past the visitors to the museum. He wandered amongst the hibiscus and bougainvillea. He didn't look at the ancestral stoneworks in the museum field. Then he went home, dazed, confused by objects, convinced that he saw many fingers pointing at him. He went down streets he had never seen in his life and he momentarily forgot where his compound was.

When he got home he found that he was trembling. He was hungry. He hadn't eaten that morning and the cupboard was empty of food. He couldn't stop thinking about the loss of his job. Anderson had suspected for some time that the supervisor had been planning to give his job to a distant relation. That was the reason why the supervisor was always berating him on the slightest pretext. Seven years in the city had begun to make Anderson feel powerless because he didn't belong to the important societies, and didn't have influential relatives. He spent the afternoon thinking about his condition in the world. He fell asleep and dreamt about his dead parents.

He woke up feeling bitter. It was late in the afternoon and he was hungry. He got out of bed and went to the market to get some beef and tripe for a pot of stew. Anderson slid through the noise of revving motors and shouting traders. He came to the goatsellers. The goats stood untethered in a small corral. As Anderson went past he had a queer feeling that the goats were staring at him. When he stopped and looked at them the animals panicked. They kicked and fought backwards. Anderson hurried on till he found himself at the meat stalls.

The air was full of flies and the stench was overpowering. He felt ill. There were intestines and bones in heaps on the floor. He was haggling the price of tripe when he heard confused howls from the section where they sold generators and videos. The meat-seller had just slapped the tripe down on the table and was telling him to go somewhere else for the price he offered, when the fire burst out with an explosion. Flames poured over the stalls. Waves of screaming people rushed in Anderson's direction. He saw the fire flowing behind them, he saw black smoke. He started to run before the people reached him.

He heard voices all around him. Dry palm fronds crackled in the air. Anderson ducked under the bare eaves of a stall, tripped over a fishmonger's basin of writhing eels, and fell into a mound of snailshells. He struggled back up. He ran past the fortune-tellers and the amulet traders. He was shouldering his way through the bamboo poles of the lace-sellers when it struck him with amazing clarity that the fire was intent upon him because he had no power to protect himself. And soon the fire was everywhere. Suddenly, from the midst of voices in the smoke, Anderson heard someone calling his names. Not just the one name, the ordinary one which made things easier in the city – Anderson; he heard all the others as well, even the ones he had forgotten: Jeremiah, Ofuegbu, Nutcracker, Azzi. He was so astonished that when he cut himself, by brushing his thigh against two rusted nails, he did not know how profusely he bled till he cleared out into the safety of the main road. When he got home he was still bleeding. When the bleeding ceased, he felt that an alien influence had insinuated itself into his body, and an illness took over.

He became so ill that most of the money he had saved in all the years of humiliation and sweat went into the hands of the quack chemists of the area. They bandaged his wound. They gave him tetanus injections with curved syringes. They gave him pills in squat, silvery bottles. Anderson was reduced to creeping about the compound, from room to toilet and back again, as though he were terrified of daylight. And then, three days into the illness, with the taste of alum stale in his mouth, he caught a glimpse of himself in the mirror. He saw the gaunt face of a complete stranger. Two days later, when he felt he had recovered sufficiently, Anderson packed his box and fled home to his village.

The Image-maker

Anderson hadn't been home for a long time. When the lorry driver dropped him at the village junction, the first things he noticed were the ferocity of the heat and the humid smell of rotting vegetation. He went down the dirt track that led to the village. A pack of dogs followed him for a short while and then disappeared. Cowhorns and the beating of drums sounded from the forest. He saw masks, eaten by insects, along the grass verge.

He was sweating when he got to the obeche tree where, during the war, soldiers had shot a woman thought to be a spy. Passing the well which used to mark the village boundary, he became aware of three rough forms running after him. They had flaming red eyes and they shouted his names.

'Anderson! Ofuegbu!'

He broke into a run. They bounded after him.

'Ofuegbu! Anderson!'

In his fear he ran so hard that his box flew open. Scattered behind him were his clothes, his medicines, and the modest gifts he had brought to show his people that he wasn't entirely a small man in the world. He discarded the box and sped on without looking back. Swirls of dust came towards him. And when he emerged from the dust, he saw the village.

It was sunset. Anderson didn't stop running till he was safely in the village. He went on till he came to the pool office with the signboard that read: MR ABAS AND CO. LICENSED COLLECTOR. Outside the office, a man sat in a depressed cane chair. His eyes stared divergently at the road and he snored gently. Anderson stood panting. He wanted to ask directions to his uncle's place, but he didn't want to wake the owner of the pool office.

Anderson wasn't sure when the man woke up, for

suddenly he said: 'Why do you have to run into our village like a madman?'

Anderson struggled for words. He was sweating.

'You disturb my eyes when you come running into our village like that.'

Anderson wiped his face. He was confused. He started to apologize, but the man looked him over once, and fell back into sleep, with his eyes still open. Anderson wasn't sure what to do. He was thirsty. With sweat dribbling down his face, Anderson tramped on through the village.

Things had changed since he'd been away. The buildings had lost their individual colours to that of the dust. Houses had moved several yards from where they used to be. Roads ran diagonally to how he remembered them. He felt he had arrived in a place he had almost never known.

Exhausted, Anderson sat on a bench outside the market. The roadside was full of ants. The heat mists made him sleepy. The market behind him was empty, but deep within it he heard celebrations and arguments. He listened to alien voices and languages from the farthest reaches of the world. Anderson fell asleep on the bench and dreamt that he was being carried through the village by the ants. He woke to find himself inside the pool office. His legs itched.

The man whom he had last seen sitting in the cane chair, was now behind the counter. He was mixing a potion of local gin and herbs. There was someone else in the office: a stocky man with a large forehead and a hardened face.

He stared at Anderson and then said: 'Have you slept enough?'

Anderson nodded. The man behind the counter came round with a tumbler full of herbal mixtures.

Almost forcing the drink down Anderson's throat, he said: 'Drink it down. Fast!'

Anderson drank most of the mixture in one gulp. It was very bitter and bile rushed up in his mouth.

'Swallow it down!'

Anderson swallowed. His head cleared a little and his legs stopped itching.

The man who had given him the drink said: 'Good.' Then he pointed to the other man and said: 'That's your uncle. Our Image-maker. Don't you remember him?'

Anderson stared at the Image-maker's face. The lights shifted. The face was elusively familiar. Anderson had to subtract seven years from the awesome starkness of the Image-maker's features before he could recognize his own uncle.

Anderson said: 'My uncle, you have changed!'

'Yes, my son, and so have you,' his uncle said.

'I'm so happy to see you,' said Anderson.

Smiling, his uncle moved into the light at the doorway. Anderson saw that his left arm was shrivelled.

'We've been expecting you,' his uncle said.

Anderson didn't know what to say. He looked from one to the other. Then suddenly he recognized Mr Abas, who used to take him fishing down the village stream.

'Mr Abas! It's you!'

'Of course it's me. Who did you think I was?'

Anderson stood up.

'Greetings, my elders. Forgive me. So much has changed.'

His uncle touched him benevolently on the shoulder and said: 'That's all right. Now, let's go.'

Anderson persisted with his greeting. Then he began to apologize for his bad memory. He told them that he had been pursued at the village boundary.

'They were strange people. They pursued me like a common criminal.'

The Image-maker said: 'Come on. Move. We don't speak of strange things in our village. We have no strange things here. Now, let's go.'

Mr Abas went outside and sat in his sunken cane chair. The Image-maker led Anderson out of the office.

They walked through the dry heat. The chanting of worshippers came from the forest. Drums and jangling bells sounded faintly in the somnolent air.

'The village is different,' Anderson said.

The Image-maker was silent.

'What has happened here?'

'Don't ask questions. In our village we will provide you with answers before it is necessary to ask questions,' the Image-maker said with some irritation.

Anderson kept quiet. As they went down the village Anderson kept looking at the Image-maker: the more he looked, the more raw and godlike the Image-maker seemed. It was as though he had achieved an independence from human agencies. He looked as if he had been cast in rock, and left to the wilds.

'The more you look, the less you see,' the Image-maker said.

It sounded, to Anderson, like a cue. They had broken into a path. Ahead of them were irregular rows of soapstone monoliths. Embossed with abstract representations of the human figure, the monoliths ranged from the babies of their breed to the abnormally large ones. There were lit candles and varied offerings in front of them. There were frangipani and iroko trees in their midst. There were also red-painted poles which had burst into flower.

His uncle said: 'The images were originally decorated with pearls, lapis lazuli, amethysts and magic glass which twinkled wonderful philosophies. But the pale ones from across the seas came and stole them. This was whispered to me in a dream.'

Anderson gazed at the oddly elegant monoliths and said: 'You resemble the gods you worship.'

His uncle gripped him suddenly.

'We don't speak of resemblances in our village, you hear?'

Anderson nodded. His uncle relaxed his grip. They moved on.

After a while his uncle said: 'The world is the shrine and the shrine is the world. Everything must have a centre. When you talk rubbish, bad things fly into your mouth.'

They passed a cluster of huts. Suddenly the Image-maker bustled forward. They had arrived at the main entrance to a circular clay shrinehouse. The Image-maker went to the niche and brought out a piece of native chalk, a tumbler and a bottle of herbs. He made a mash which he smeared across Anderson's forehead. On a nail above the door, there was a bell which the Image-maker rang three times.

A voice called from within the hut.

The Image-maker sprayed himself forth in a list of his incredible names and titles. Then he requested permission to bring to the shrine an afflicted 'son of the soil'.

The voices asked if the 'son of the soil' was ready to come in.

The Image-maker was silent.

A confusion of drums, bells, cowhorns, came suddenly from within. Anderson fainted.

Then the Image-maker said to the voices: 'He is ready to enter!'

They came out and found that Anderson was light.

They bundled him into the shrinehouse and laid him on a bed of congealed palm oil.

The Image

When Anderson came to he could smell burning candles, sweat and incense. Before him was the master Image, a hallucinatory warrior monolith decorated in its original splendour of precious stones and twinkling glass. At its base were roots, kola nuts and feathers. When Anderson gazed at the master Image he heard voices that were not spoken and he felt drowsiness come over him.

Candles burned in the mist of blue incense. A small crowd of worshippers danced and wove Anderson's names in songs. Down the corridors he could hear other supplicants crying out in prayer for their heart's desires, for their afflictions and problems. They prayed like people who are ill and who are never sure of recovering. It occurred to Anderson that it must be a cruel world to demand such intensity of prayer.

Anderson tried to get up from the bed, but couldn't. The master Image seemed to look upon him with a grotesque face. The ministrants closed in around him. They praised the master Image in songs. The Image-maker gave a sudden instruction and the ministrants rushed to Anderson. They spread out their multiplicity of arms and embraced Anderson in their hard compassions. But when they touched Anderson he screamed and shouted in hysteria. The ministrants embraced him with their remorseless arms and carried him through the corridors and out into the night. They rushed him past the monoliths outside. They took him past creeks and waterholes. When they came to a blooming frangipani tree, they dumped him on the ground. Then they retreated with flutters of their smocks, and disappeared as though the darkness were made of their own substance.

Anderson heard whispers in the forest. He heard things falling among the branches. Then he heard footsteps that seemed for ever approaching. He soon saw that it was Mr Abas. He carried a bucket in one hand and a lamp in the other. He dropped the bucket near Anderson.

'Bathe of it,' Mr Abas said, and returned the way he had come.

Anderson washed himself with the treated water. When he finished the attendants came and brought him fresh clothes. Then they led him back to the shrine-house.

The Image-maker was waiting for him. Bustling with urgency, his bad arm moving restlessly like the special instrument of his functions, the Image-maker grabbed Anderson and led him to an alcove.

He made Anderson sit in front of a door. There was a hole greased with palm oil at the bottom of the door. The Image-maker shouted an instruction and the attendants came upon Anderson and held him face down. They pushed him towards the hole; they forced his head and shoulders through it.

In the pain Anderson heard the Image-maker say: 'Tell us what you see!'

Anderson couldn't see anything. All he could feel was the grinding pain. Then he saw a towering tree. There was a door on the tree trunk. Then he saw a thick blue pall. A woman emerged from the pall. She was painted over in native chalk. She had bangles all the way up her arms. Her stomach and waist were covered in beads.

'I see a woman,' he cried.

Several voices asked: 'Do you know her?'
'No.'
'Is she following you?'
'I don't know.'
'Is she dead?'
'I don't know.'
'Is she dead?'
'No!'
There was the merriment of tinkling bells.
'What is she doing?'
She had come to the tree and opened the door. Anderson suffered a fresh agony. She opened a second door and tried the third one, but it didn't open. She tried again and when it gave way with a crash Anderson finally came through – but he lost consciousness.

Afterwards, they fed him substantially. Then he was allowed the freedom to move round the village and visit some of his relations. In the morning the Image-maker sent for him. The attendants made him sit on a cowhide mat and they shaved off his hair. They lit red and green candles and made music around him. Then the Image-maker proceeded with the extraction of impurities from his body. He rubbed herbal juices into Anderson's shoulder. He bit into the flesh and pulled out a rusted little padlock which he spat into an enamel bowl. He inspected the padlock. After he had washed out his mouth, he bit into Anderson's shoulder again and pulled out a crooked needle. He continued like this till he had pulled out a piece of broken glass, a twisted nail, a cowrie, and a small key. There was some agitation as to whether the key would fit the padlock, but it didn't.

When the Image-maker had finished he picked up the bowl, jangled the objects, and said: 'All these things, where do they come from? Who sent them into you?'

Anderson couldn't say anything.

The Image-maker went on to cut light razor strokes on Anderson's arm and he rubbed protective herbs into the bleeding marks. He washed his hands and went out of the alcove. He came back with a pouch, which he gave to Anderson with precise instructions of its usage.

Then he said: 'You are going back to the city tomorrow. Go to your place of work, collect the money they are owing you, and look for another job. You will have no trouble. You understand?'

Anderson nodded.

'Now, listen. One day I went deep into the forest because my arm hurt. I injured it working in a factory. For three days I was in the forest praying to our ancestors. I ate leaves and fishes. On the fourth day I forgot how I came there. I was lost and everything was new to me. On the fifth day I found the Images. They were hidden amongst the trees and tall grasses. Snakes and tortoises were all around. My pain stopped. When I found my way back and told the elders of the village what I had seen they did not believe me. The Images had been talked about in the village for a long time but no one had actually seen them. That is why they made me the Image-maker.'

He paused, then continued.

'Every year, around this time, spirits from all over the world come to our village. They meet at the marketplace and have heated discussions about everything under the sun. Sometimes they gather round our Images outside. On some evenings there are purple mists round the iroko tree. At night we listen to all the languages, all the philosophies, of the world. You must come home now and again. This is where you derive power. You hear?'

Anderson nodded. He hadn't heard most of what was said. He had been staring at the objects in the enamel bowl.

The Image-eaters

Anderson ate little through the ceremonies that followed the purification of his body. After all the dancing and feasting to the music of cowhorns and tinkling bells, they made him lie down before the master Image. Then the strangest voice he had ever heard thundered the entire shrinehouse with its full volume.

'ANDERSON! OFUEGBU! YOU ARE A SMALL MAN. YOU CANNOT RUN FROM YOUR FUTURE. GOVERNMENTS CANNOT EXIST WITHOUT YOU. ALL THE DISASTERS OF THE WORLD REST ON YOU AND HAVE YOUR NAME. THIS IS YOUR POWER.'

The ministrants gave thanks and wept for joy.

Anderson spent the night in the presence of the master Image. He dreamt that he was dying of hunger and that there was nothing left in the world to eat. When Anderson ate of the master Image he was surprised at its sweetness. He was surprised also that the Image replenished itself.

In the morning Anderson's stomach was bloated with an imponderable weight. Shortly before his departure the Image-maker came to him and suggested that he contribute to the shrine fund. When Anderson made his donation, the Image-maker gave his blessing. The ministrants prayed for him and sang of his destiny.

Anderson had just enough money to get him back to the city. When he was ready to leave, Anderson felt a new heaviness come upon him. He thanked his uncle for everything and made his way through the village.

He stopped at the pool office. Mr Abas was in his

sunken cane chair, his eyes pursuing their separate lines of vision. Anderson wasn't sure if Mr Abas was asleep.

He said: 'I'm leaving now.'

'Leaving us to our hunger, are you?'

'There is hunger where I am going,' Anderson said.

Mr Abas smiled and said: 'Keep your heart pure. Have courage. Suffering cannot kill us. And travel well.'

'Thank you.'

Mr Abas nodded and soon began to snore. Anderson went on towards the junction.

As he walked through the heated gravity of the village Anderson felt like an old man. He felt that his face had stiffened. He had crossed the rubber plantation, had crossed the boundary, and was approaching the junction, when the rough forms with blazing eyes fell upon him. He fought them off. He lashed out with his stiffened hands and legs. They could easily have torn him to pieces, because their ferocity was greater than his. There was a moment in which he saw himself dead. But they suddenly stopped and stared at him. Then they pawed him, as though he had become allied with them in some way. When they melted back into the heat mists, Anderson experienced the new simplicity of his life, and continued with his journey.

Masquerades

I

THE LIGHTS WERE cut as he pushed his way up the slope. The air was fresh and there was the sweet smell of earth after rain. He climbed the slope high enough for him to see the front of his compound and then he made for the cover of a banana plant. Insects thrilled from the forest and all around him. In the darkness he watched the house. The two men were still there.

One of them sat on a stool and smoked a cigarette and gazed at the forest. His companion had one foot shorter than the other and had taken to limping up and down the forecourt. They both clapped at mosquitoes. Fireflies darted around them.

Watching the men from behind the plant, he brought out the little bottle of Arabian perfume he always carried with him. He slapped a good quantity on his neck and shirtfront. The men looked as though they would be waiting for some time. It was his night off and he decided to go and have a few drinks. He carefully made his way down the wet slope.

He had passed the woman at the crossroad, who sold fried bean cakes and fish, when the lights came back on.

Music came on too at the hotel. As he approached he
could see the prostitutes in the dark places of the street.
They called out to potential customers. He didn't see any
of the women that he knew. He went into the hotel,
where raw music poured out from faulty loudspeakers,
and he spent the next three hours getting drunk.

He sat on a straight-backed chair. He had five bottles of
beer and a glass on the table. It was very crowded in the
hotel. Three women danced in semi-nudity on the stage.
He listened to the drunken disc jockey screeching above
the music. On the walls there were murals of fat women
entangled with thin men in dark glasses. The last time he
had been to the hotel was a few weeks back, when a fight
had broken out and a man got slashed at the throat by
one of the new prostitutes.

   The noise of the singing crowd, the flashing lights and
grating music, started a throbbing in his eyes. He drank
steadily. The more he drank the more melancholy he
became. His neck began to hurt again. And he kept seeing
the two men waiting at the bottom of each glass of beer.

   Women conspicuously brushed past his table. One of
them smiled cunningly at him as she went past. She had
sheen above her eyes. She was robust and fleshy and
wore a tight-fitting dress. He was sweating. He smiled
back at her. She came and sat next to him and she moved
with the music. He slapped on some more of his perfume.

   'What's your name?'

   'Titi.'

   She had small bright hungry eyes and large breasts.
She kept rearranging her dress.

   'What do you want to drink?'

   'Guinness,' she said.

   He got up and fought his way through the crowd.
After a while he came back with three more bottles of

beer and two bottles of Guinness. He drank steadily. He didn't pay much attention to her, but he could feel her restlessness. He could also feel her eyes roving languidly over the bustling dancefloor.

'You don't like me?' she asked, teasingly.

He didn't say anything.

'Or is ya prick small? It doesn't matter. The size doesn't matter.'

'What's your business with my prick?'

'Come, let's dance. You're too quiet.'

He laughed, and she stood up. She looked bored. She straightened her dress down her knees and then she looked at her face in the mirror behind them. He studied her. He looked at her from her legs upwards and when he got to her face he was surprised at the supreme boredom of her expression. Soon they were dancing.

It was rowdy on the dancefloor. Drinks had been spilt and the ground was slippery. Couples collided into one another, some fell over tables, pushed by the violent dancing of the crowd. The three semi-nude women were still on stage; they looked tired and their faces sagged.

Titi was a much better dancer than he was. She moved freely. She shook her body and threw her arms in joyful abandon. When he saw her wet armpits he smiled. He swayed on the ball of drunkenness and forced an elated mood to take over the evening. He was seriously out of rhythm with the music and he noticed that she was getting increasingly sexual in her dance. She had brought her hips against his groin. When he held her sweating body close he could feel her flesh vibrating against his restraint. The music went soft and she pressed herself closer to him. She moved with such purposefulness that he felt she was squashing his testicles. Then the music went faster. The drunken disc jockey talked loud over the music and Titi jumped up. In her excitement she stepped on his toes with the sharp end of her heels. He howled and staggered back; people pushed him forward; and she caught him in her arms with a smile. He was still angry and was about to throw her off when he felt her deftly reaching down. She flicked him and he stopped. He looked at her and then made for their table. He drank his way through a bottle of beer. He wiped the sweat off his face. He applied some perfume to his hair. He creaked his neck. Then he asked her to come home with him.

She hedged. She made excuses. She took a deliberate interest in other men. She laughed louder and more publicly as he grew more possessive. Fighting the depression which rose from his stomach he offered more drinks, some fried chicken, meat pies. She offered to go and buy them. He noticed that she kept the change.

'Why do you have all this perfume on you?'

He ignored the question. When a highlife record came on he got up and dragged her to the dancefloor and he danced his depression into a bygone era. He was beginning to enjoy himself, to find his mood, when she announced that she had to go, and that he was wasting the time. It became necessary for prices to be discussed. He proposed four naira. She didn't argue; she only insisted on changing her clothes. When she left he danced for a while, but without elation.

He went outside to cool down. When she reappeared he saw her in the moonlight and she looked different. She had changed into a mini-dress and red high-heeled shoes. She had a little blue bag over her shoulder. She wasn't as youthful as he had thought. She had a crumpled face and her figure was generous only around her buttocks. Her legs were quite stout. But the fresh air sharpened his intoxication and he walked drunkely. He held her close to him. He sang highlife. She walked with a tired lilt.

They passed the woman who sold fried bean cakes and

fish. She was closing up for the night; her smouldering fire lit up her face and illuminated the midges. He stopped singing as they went up the slope; and before they got to the top the lights were cut. It was suddenly dark and all over the area he could hear the children shouting. Kerosene lamps came on in the houses. The moon shone thinly on the rusted zinc rooftops. At the top of the slope he saw that the two men were smoking in the darkness.

He said to the woman: 'Go into that house and wait for me in the corridor. If those men ask you anything tell them to mind their own business, you hear?'

'Why? What kind of trick is this?'

In a rising voice, he said: 'Just go. And don't ask foolish questions.'

She brought out a cigarette from her bag.

'And don't light any cigarettes, you hear?'

She muttered something, but she went. He watched her swaying. He watched her as she passed the two men. They said something to her and he saw her angry gestures as she shouted something back at them. When she disappeared into the corridor and the two men didn't go after her, he went to the house by way of the backyards. In the darkness he walked into buckets and stoves that had been left out. He paused to urinate against the bamboo tree near the window of his room. When he finished he brought out a penknife from his pocket and opened the wooden window; he climbed in quickly and shut it behind him. He opened the door, stuck his head out, and called her softly in the darkness. Fireflies came in with her.

'Close the door quick,' he said.

'Why all this?'

'Lower your voice. Shut the door. I don't want any mosquitoes.'

Shutting the door, she said: 'You think you're so special that mosquitoes won't bite you?'

'Lock the door,' he said.

She locked it with the key. She couldn't see him. She stood near the door and the smells of lavender and jasmine came to her nostrils. She also smelt perfumed soaps, camphor, clean sheets, new clothes, leather, and velvet materials. The room was cool as mint. When he lit the lamp she looked round and drew her breath. It was as if she had materialized in the splendour of a curious slum paradise. The walls were blue. A plastic chandelier hung down from the ceiling. There were several large photographs of him on the walls, along with posters of London and Paris, Brazil with its Sango dancers, America with a saloon scene from the Wild West. She saw hats on nails. She looked into the open wardrobe near the door and saw his white coats, terylene suits, his bow ties, his walking stick and several umbrellas. He had sunglasses, a clutter of shoes, a bathrobe and two wigs. There were Correspondence Courses littering the floor. There were two glass cabinets in the room: one contained plates, cutlery and plastic flowers; the other had glittering modest stereo equipment. Taking up most of the space was a family-sized bed. Mosquito nettings trailed down and had been tucked neatly under the mattress. There was a Benin mask above the door; next to it was a picture of Jesus Christ. Directly opposite, above the window, was a piece of antelope skin. There was a chair, a sofa and a stool.

'Sit down,' he said.

'Is this ya place?' she asked, as she passed a long mirror on one side of the wardrobe.

'Sit down. Of course it's my place.'

She came back and looked at herself in the mirror. Then she sat on the sofa. He sat on the chair. He saw that her stomach bulged against her dress. Her lips had a cynical smile that would never leave. Beneath the glitter of her sheen she had red eyes, with one narrower than the other. Her cheeks were mottled.

'Don't you give people drinks?' she said, crossing her legs. The mini-dress rode her thighs and he saw her pants. He saw also that she had the beginnings of a rash. He got up and went to the fridge, hidden behind the bed, and brought out two bottles of bedewed beer and a bottle of Guinness. He put them on the centre table.

He said: 'I have plenty of drinks, but why should I give you any?'

She was quiet; then she laughed and said: 'What business are you in?'

'What's your business with my business?'

'You be spy or something like dat?' she said, uncrossing her legs. She brought out a chewing gum from her bag and folded it into her mouth.

'I will kick you out if you don't shut up, you hear?'

She looked at him for a long moment before she said: 'What did you bring me here for? If you want to do it, let's do it and let me go. I have other customers, you know.'

'I know,' he said.

He got up and brought out a little tape-recorder from under the bed. He started to play something and then he stopped. He pushed it back under.

'Have you got some Jimmy Cliff?'

'No.'

'Put on some highlife. Let's dance.'

'No.'

'What kind of business do you do?'

He didn't say anything. He got up from the chair, dragged out a section of the netting from under the mattress, and sat on the bed. The bedspread was of satin, the pillowcase was of velvet. He was sweating. She scratched her thighs.

'Why don't you want to talk?'

'Keep quiet,' he said. He was listening out for something, his head craned in the direction of the door.

Outside, a fowl stirred on the branches of a bamboo tree.
A dog howled and the sound seemed to come from the
rooftops. Somewhere in the backyard a woman sang in a
crackling voice.

At the front of the house the two men were becoming
restless. They had seen the lights come and go; they had
smoked several cigarettes. They leant against the wall
and watched the fowls curled up on the branches.

'This is not the sort of area to live in,' the man with the
limp said suddenly.

'Too dirty,' said the other.

'All you can smell is shit.'

'Too many mosquitoes.'

They were quiet for a moment.

'I'm going to build a house in the village one day.'

'I'll build one in the city.'

'Too much trouble in the city.'

'Where there's trouble there's money.'

'I'm getting tired of this kind of life,' said the one with
the limp. He lit a cigarette.

'You can quit but you have to run far.'

'I'm not quitting. I'm just tired.'

They both watched a car that had turned the corner
and was coughing its way towards the slope. It stalled as
it passed them. The driver stuck his head out of the
window and asked them to help push the car.

'Where are you going?' said the man with the limp.

'Down that slope.'

'How much?'

'Help me push it. Out of charity.'

'Charity is not free.'

'One naira.'

'Give us the money first.'

'All right,' the driver said. The two men went over. The man with the limp took the money. They pushed the car down the slope and when it started they went back to the house. They shared the money.

The other man said: 'Let's go and see if he's in.'

They went into the corridor and towards his room.

II

Inside, he had been finding the woman's legs too heavy to hold in the crook of both arms. He moved on her vigorously, but unsatisfactorily. He tried not to make any noise. Now and again the bed creaked. He sweated. He panted quietly. She did not sweat. She watched the fireflies that had got into the netting. She chewed on her bubble gum. She occasionally slapped mosquitoes. When she expertly moved her hips, he groaned. He was gaining her depths, ecstatically, when the first knocks sounded on the door. He stopped, but it was too late. He came while the knocking increased.

He lay still. He listened to them calling out if anyone was in. He heard them asking a neighbour of his whereabouts. The neighbour couldn't help. No one in the compound knew anything about him. The woman moved on the bed, creaking it slightly, when they knocked again. He motioned her to be quiet. She blew out a little balloon with her bubble gum. After a while he heard their footsteps recede down the corridor.

He rolled off her and got out of bed. He tied on a wrapper and sprayed the room with a can of air freshener. She climbed out of bed and got dressed. He paid her; she counted the money and put it away in her brassiere. Then he asked her to go. She looked at him, smiling and asked if he didn't want any more. She glanced round the room. He got up from the chair and pushed her towards the window.

'You want me to go through here?'

'Yes.'

'I didn't come through the window. I can't go out through the window. Am I a thief?'

'Just go,' he said.

'Something is wrong with ya head.'

'My head is my own problem.'

'What happened to the door?'

'Didn't you hear the people knocking?'

'So? Is it my problem?'

'Go, you hear? Make you begin go,' he said, his voice rising.

She picked up her bag, pushed past him, opened the door, and went out. The two men saw her emerge from the corridor.

The man with the limp nudged the other one and then he said: 'Woman, where are you coming from? Where are you going?'

She went past, clacking her heels, rolling her backside. The man with the limp got up and followed her. He was shorter than she was. When she got to the edge of the slope she turned suddenly and lashed him with her bag. She hit him on the head. He laughed. She dropped her bag and took off her shoes. She grabbed his arms and wrestled with him. She lifted him up and threw him, face down, on the ground. His friend watched them; he smoked stolidly. The man with the limp got up. She waited a moment before she hit him over the head with one of her heels. Then she snatched up her bag and shoes and sped down the slope. She disappeared behind a house where a kerosene lamp burned steadily on a stall. The man with the limp made his way back to the house. His companion laughed.

'Why are you laughing?' ˙

'You've got mud all over you.'

'Yes, but look.'

He had some crumpled naira notes in his hand. His companion laughed again. The man with the limp put the money in his breast pocket and sat down on the stool. He looked towards the forest. There was a glow in the sky.

When she had gone he went out through the window. He went to the bathroom and washed himself. He came back in and blew out the hurricane lantern. He soon fell asleep. He dreamt about the strange man who had come up to him outside his work premises. The man didn't have a nose in the dream. The man asked him to dump a bucket of shit in front of an enemy's house. The man paid him generously, but when he looked at the money afterwards he saw nothing in his hands except some wood shaving. He started to shout and he woke up. He soon slept again. In another dream people were running after him. They all limped. He ran down into a market and mingled with a band of masquerades. Then suddenly he was the masquerade. He was the dancer in the market square. He had a mighty mask on his face, he walked on stilts, and he carried a basket of fruits. He was dancing alone.

When he woke up early in the afternoon, it had rained, and the men had gone. When he went to work at night there was no one waiting for him there either. At the backhouse he changed his clothes; he wore the stinking work garb. He swathed his face and neck with fresh sacking. He got on the waiting truck with his silent colleagues. The city glowered and the truck bounced them through the potholed streets and wild roads, through the areas he had come to know like a wound.

III

It stank on the truck. Maggots, which had escaped the cursory disinfectant washing, slithered up the sides of the woodwork. Cockroaches crawled around on the tailboard. The buckets rattled against one another. Next to him, a colleague sat on the truck's metal grid. The driver of the truck pursued a Mercedes Benz without much success. They soon came to the area where the night's work was to begin.

When they jumped off the truck they dispersed into the confusion of streets and went to the backyards of various houses. They came out from the back of the toilets with buckets on their heads. They staggered to the trucks and grunted when they deposited the buckets. The truck moved on to catch up with them.

And then he was momentarily lost. He had come out from the gap between houses and the bucket was almost unbearably heavy on his head. The truck had gone. He staggered down the labyrinthine streets with his head raw and his neck burning. He heard drums. He heard a lorry blast its horn. He came to a clearing and found himself confronting three fearful masquerades. They danced with menacing vigour, stamping and shaking the ground. They made frightening noises amidst the drums and bells surrounding them.

Unable to control the weight on his bursting head, he pitched forward. Suddenly he heard the rustle and tearing of bamboo filigrees. He heard the drums fall and the voices break into screams. Soon there was no one around. He half-ran, half-buckled down the street; and he came to a junction where, to his great relief, the truck was waiting.

IV

He was at the hotel. He had on a bedraggled French suit and wore an imitation gold chain round his neck. He was sweating. It was noisy in the hotel. Many of the men wore dark glasses. He was talking to the prostitute. He was talking very loud and he kept opening his mouth very wide. He was quite drunk and his neck hurt badly.

He was saying: 'I have seen all kinds of things. I am not afraid of anybody. When I look at people I see nothing. What doesn't turn to shit turns to dust.'

He looked around. The woman stared at him. Her face didn't move.

'You have to pay me for the money they took. And for my heels.'

'Why?'

'What kind of question is that? Those two friends of yours took my money. That's why I don't like strange customers.'

'Okay. How much?'

'Four naira.'

'I will give it to you.'

'When?'

He ignored her. He brought out his bottle of perfume and slapped some on his face.

'What kind of perfume is that?'

'Moon of Arabia.'

He looked at the musicians performing on stage.

'So tell me, what kind of business are you in?'

He glared at her. He waved his hands.

He said: 'You want to know my business?' He laughed. Sweat poured down his forehead. He said: 'One day a man came to me. He said I should dump such and such in front of such and such a man's house. Why should I? Because of money, that's why. So I took the money and then I went and forgot the address and I had to dump the thing in front of the house of the man who paid me. What could I do? You want to know my business? Money business. Just like you. Everything na shit unless you get money. Dat's what I think.'

His perfume stank the place out. He became quite grim. He was so drunk that all he saw around him were the figures of masquerades invading the city.

Looking at the musicians, he said: 'When a man blows his trumpet he must drink water.'

'You talk nonsense,' she said.

Smiling, he said: 'Come home with me.'

'Why? You haven't paid me for . . .'

'All right.'

He counted out four naira and gave them to her.

'Let's go home,' he said again.

She put the money in her brassiere. Her eyes were bitter. The edges of her mouth were turned down.

'No,' she said, finally.

'Maybe tomorrow?'

'Maybe.'

He got up and left; his head was at an angle.

When he got to the housefront he saw that the people of his compound were gathered along the road. He felt the unforgiving accusation of their gaze. The two men weren't there. As he hurried down the corridor he noticed a familiar pungency in the air. His door had been kicked open. When he put on the light his drunkenness immediately left him. It was with a terrible clarity that he saw the bucket on his centre table. He ran out of his room and staggered to the housefront. He sat on a stool. Midges flew around his head. There was still the sweetness of earth after rain, but no one could have noticed.

A Hidden History

and because nothing can be hidden from memory the houses in the street were in ruins. The last inhabitants were immigrants from lands whose destinies had been altered by slavery. They had come, answering the call of their former rulers, to be menials of society. When they first arrived they brought laughter to the street. They thought a wider world had opened to them. The sun on the pavement, glittering bits of broken glass, dazzled their vision. After that first breath of the spring air, that early wonder, their sensations would never be so pure.

and children were born; they grew up in the street; the world did not want them. On weekends they played football and listened to popular music through the open windows. The men bought secondhand cars (which never travelled far) and washed them with the family on Saturdays. On Sundays they painted the doors, tended the drooping flowers in the pots, and worshipped different gods. They made friendships which did not last when the troubles came. They built little wooden gates in front of their houses.

and all that time the inhabitants thought the world was growing bigger, it was actually being made smaller. The invisible places of the country soon located them. One morning they all received letters from the government. They read the letters, saw incomprehensible shapes of the future, and kept quiet. They had solitary Christmases that year.

the winter was hardly over when two demolition hulks were implanted at the mouth of the street. The secondhand cars were sold off. Shadows lengthened on the street, music ceased coming from the windows, and the children didn't come out to play. Some of the houses had their electricity cut and rising damp grew wild on the walls. The houses which all those years had been sinking into decrepitude, were mysteriously quickened into rot. People were seen only in the mornings, when the mists were heavy and grey; or at night, when they wound complicated routes to avoid it being known that they lived in a street that was being effaced from memory. The inhabitants began to look out despairingly from behind their windows. I saw them sometimes, their faces squashed together, staring bewildered at the advancement of the tower blocks.

then one by one – shamefully, like a disgraced people – they left. Vacated houses were quickly boarded up and fenced round with corrugated zinc. Street lamps stopped functioning. It was just as well, for it became unnecessary for them to pretend they did not see one another. Those that stayed watched as those from other places emptied their rubbish at the mouth of the street. The demolition hulks grew rust. The metal balls grew heavier in the air.

then came the mob from the tower blocks and from other places in the city, a generation that would not find employment. They discovered the street and its last remaining inhabitants. They burned down one of the houses and experimented with two others. The mob, however, was not the real reason for the increased disappearance of the street's inhabitants. They had to leave, every single one of them, because a monstrous negative force rose from the wild gardens of all the rotting houses. The children imagined all kinds of sounds in the street and the men dreamed of metal balls that were as large as the sky. The children and women stayed awake most nights because the street had become the repository of all the invisible hatred of all those who lived around, and who dreamed of a large playground for their children and a pond in the middle so the children could sometimes see their reflections.

when the last of them left (with their large families) I watched from the window and saw them in the chill of morning as they scuttled between house and road, carrying their radiograms, boxes of clothes, photo albums, and some chinoiserie. There was a lorry waiting to take them away. I went down among them, to console them. When they saw me they gave a gasp of horror. Had I been away for so long? Afraid that I might make their burden heavier, I passed on. They packed quickly and nervously. The lorries took them away. They had forgotten the dreams that brought them here. The roads they would walk on were paved with blood: how could they have thought of it as gold?

after they left the rats discovered the street. When the rats found the gardens, the empty rotting houses, the cupboards infested with the purple of long-leftover food, they rejoiced. They screeched loudly in the discovery of so hidden a universe, of pastures so rich.

the hatred of all those who grew more imprisoned within the advancing towers did not stop when the inhabitants disappeared. They hated the street even more ferociously because it was now devoid of the brand of human content that they had worked so hard to efface.

Vengefully, they brought their rubbish to the empty street. Packs of dogs were encouraged by canophiles to excrete there to their hearts' content. Many of the dogs that came there were mangy, their tails stood up stiff, and they had no owners. I often watched the dogs that never formed alliances, that always ran along on their own, their eyes sly, their tails quick to noise. I went among them sometimes and found them a generally quite trusting bunch of individuals. Gangs of humans came there too. They turned the street into their initiation ground. They excreted from place to place along the street. They threw things at one another. They never forgot to curse the former inhabitants, as though they were still living in the street. I passed among them sometimes. They ignored me.

the birds came too. They wheeled in the air and alighted on the street. Ravens, crows and starlings: there were so many of them sometimes that there wouldn't be a single visible place on the street and rooftops besides their restless shapes. They often managed to infest the rubbish mounds with vibrant life. When they departed, flapping their wings and beating spirals of feathers into the air, they left the street and rooftops beneath them covered in mottled white, the true purpose of their visits.

then the demolition hulks were retrieved from the garbage: there seemed to be no more interest in destroying the street, which was left to fester. Those who came to dump their rubbish there never needed to look, to see the uneven humps of rubbish formation, nor did they ever need to imagine the pressure of refuse on refuse, compressing into some unknown substance or slime: the distilled liquids of the street.

sulphurous smells rose from this festeration. Pink mushrooms sprouted. Strange vegetable life took root beneath the rubbish and spread wings in the nights and grew rings round the street. Then this vegetable life flowered into purple and green flora, beautiful to look at like the fata morgana with terrible blue eyes, but they gave off corrosive smells that drove the dogs to a restricted area of the street: to the area that I dwell in, earthbound. To see the festerations flower, to see them bloom, and to see what they flowered from, what liquids, to see this from one night to another: this is the vision at the heart of nightmare.

from the tower blocks that surrounded the street came the sound of continuous wailing. Babies cried loud into the most serene mornings. Men and women sometimes threw themselves down from the heights and smashed their bodies on the cement lawns. Everywhere they cried for a space free from history. The towers advanced. The street stayed fetid.

and then!

one night a silver chill hung over the street. Several people went past, away from the towers. Who were they? What new exodus did they represent? They grumbled and cursed. Green mists formed when they breathed. Had they come up with a new use for their neglect? They didn't stop and didn't look. I saw that not one of them could hold his dignity in the midst of the sunken street.

not one of them!

sometimes I could hear the rain before it pattered on the broken pavements. That night it rained. Silvery drops slanted and washed down hard on the street. It was difficult to see into the rain. It was on such nights that I felt the burden of being earthbound, having to see it all in every grain and not see very far at all. Yes, the rain slanted. The rain force came beating down and disintegrating streams crashed on the rooftops. The house shook, a section of the walls collapsed behind me. It rained beyond the dreams of the season. It struck me that cosmic phenomena – the indifferent thing at the centre of boundless love – also has a function on this, the most forgotten planet of them all. What rain it was! How it poured down so all you could see was water! The street flooded. Unable to flow anywhere else, it became a lake harbouring its own putrefaction.

the following morning I saw that the tiles of the roof-tops had gone. Some of the houses had crumbled. The street lamps had been beaten almost parallel with the ground. When the water drained away, the street was washed brilliantly clean. Rain clean. And the rubbish heaps? They were all over the entrance. The street was blocked off with the soggy pilings of rubbish stacked so high that my immolation seemed complete.

I was wrong. Later that day I heard a curious annun-ciation: the coughing of a car engine. Then the sound, agonized and insistent, climbed the refuse. Then it came from on high, from the rooftops, or from the heavens. It soon became clear that someone was having great difficulty dislodging mucus from his nose, as well as great persistence. Soon he burst into song, a dreadful song. He struck me as one who never sang at all. In this most unmysterious of places, he had rediscovered a use for his unmelodic voice. I looked out of the window. Set against the skyline, like an apocalyptic scarecrow, a ragged figure from the end of time, was the man whom I named the List-maker.

he was a squat man. He had thin wisps of black hair. He clambered down from the heights of refuse, bringing wet rubbish upon his head. He took measured strides along the street. He must have fancied himself the discoverer of a new city. He saw the street in a much cleaner condition than it had ever known, so I could forgive the ecstasy which seemed to possess him. I almost envied him the discovery of a place that seemed new, a fresh slate on which he could scratch his nature.

one of his eyes was clotted, the other one twitched. He took an abnormal interest in material things like stones, corals, broken glass, rubbish linings (regardless of their condition and what they contained), hardened – indeed, fossilized – pieces of dogshit. He listened to these objects, smelt them, laughed at them. He found himself somewhere to live in the back rooms of a half-crumbled house. If he was mad it was not in the Africa in his mind that he was mad.

of all earthly creatures, only fleas have the capacity to irritate my insubstantial nature. There were no fleas before. He brought them. The smell of rats came from him every morning. He would shake out his coat with the first blessed light of dawn. The clouds which material-ized from that coat took the form of wingless nightmares and haunted me. When the urge seized him he would thrash his coat on the street, whip it on the lamp posts, or he would swing it round his head in the air like a monstrous lasso. He created such a din that I sometimes waited excitedly for his own terrible cloud of filth to take on a centrifugal force and swing him away. It never happened.

and he stayed.

and because of him the birds, which brought flight and wondrous gliding, stopped coming. The street dogs also stopped. Even animals fear the smell of madness.

the world did try to reach us. They hacked through and climbed over the mountainous entanglement of rot. When the explorers set eyes on the List-maker they proceeded to beat him up. They turned out to be a later generation of mobs from the tower blocks and other places in the city, a generation that would not find employment. They had inherited the myth of the street of hate. They drove the List-maker into a corner.

every new day the List-maker forgot that the street was no longer his to investigate, to wander around in its labyrinths. He didn't notice that he was in a new situation of danger. It was when they took to stoning him from the top of the mountainous refuse that I first heard him laughing and crying in a new insanity. To console him, I paid a visit.

hundreds of big dark rats with paranoid eyes and long tails scattered themselves as I came in. The walls of the List-maker's abode were covered in green and grey fungus. The cracks in the walls spread like an annotated illumination of arteries. The ceiling was profuse with sentient mushrooms. Jasmines and chrysanthemums, long left to rot, stank from the bog-waste of the gardens. Christmas trees grown abnormally large twisted with weeping willows and ivy. His domain wearied me. I was anxious to leave. In the next room I heard him cough and blow his nose (insistently, and with courage). I sped on, anxious to leave, for it was doubly earthbound being there. I went into his room. His twitching eye gave a sour look in my direction. The itch seized him: he found his coat, thrashed it insanely on the floor and walls and drove me away.

sometimes when he thought his antagonists weren't around he would roam the street again: up and down, round and round, crawling about in imaginary cellars. But they watched him silently from the top of the refuse and they saw him as he made invisible lists and investigated every rubbish lining. Then one day they posted a rubbish bin lining for him to investigate. They left it in the middle of the street.

they watched him from the top of the refuse. They watched him remembering that he was of the devil, cursed in the Bible; that his sperm was black, that he was descendant of an ape; remembering that he was one of those who tainted, took their jobs and their fathers' jobs, took their women; and that he had a member big enough to shame the human race.

they held their breath as they watched him going up and down, circling inevitably towards the rubbish bin lining. He got to the lining and opened it and dipped his hand in. His eye twitched. He brought out a bloodied leg: its toes were big and blue-black with a strange rot of the feet. He brought out a hand that was gnarled and withered like a twig. He brought out an arm chopped off at the shoulder, dangling a sticky mess of blood vessels and nerves. Then he brought out the head of a black woman, roughly hacked, the eyes open and bloated, the nose cut like a harelip that had repeated itself. He brought them out, smelling, listening, thorough in his investigation. He was drawn by the temptation to list.

his antagonists watched him from the refuse. Their faces had turned red with extraordinarily suppressed animation.

the List-maker fixedly examined the parts of the woman's body. He tried to fit them into a coherent picture, a thing, and it seemed his memory utterly failed him. I hurried down. Why? What could I do? When I got to the street he had already put the parts of the woman back into the lining. His eyes had gone strange: they no longer seemed to have any connection with his head. He pushed past, dragging the burdened lining behind him. He went round and round, in zigs and zags. I watched him for a sign of how long I would be condemned in this prison of a street that was always made new, and with the old things seeping from underneath.

suddenly one of his antagonists on the refuse threw up. Another one threw up as well, convulsively. Then they all fell to vomiting. They scrambled down the refuse and they were throwing up and choking all the way into the distance.

the List-maker tried to fit the pieces of the woman's body into a remembered shape. He tried for a long time. After a while he no longer appeared on the street. I went searching for him. He was nowhere to be found. The street seemed to have entirely swallowed him.

afterwards they came and demolished what was left standing of the crumbled houses. It was all so much that, with all my burden, I asked for a clear sky and a warm little sun like a golden eye always seeing. I slept. It rained a thousand times and sunned a thousand others in the long spaces of that sleep. I awoke as black an angel as I've always been, my wings heavy and black like all the sin they make me carry in their language.

the tower blocks had been replaced with gigantic ones. The sky was fiery. The sun had moved permanently closer. The gigantic tower blocks were empty. At night I could hear only the cats wailing in ecstasy over the city. Nothing can be pushed beneath the surface of memory. There was a green lake where the street had been.

Crooked Prayer

W HEN I GAVE the note to Uncle Saba he seemed to age suddenly before my eyes. He blew out his cheeks and looked in the distance above my head.

'When did she give it to you?' he asked after a while.

'This evening. She said I should wait until your wife wasn't around.'

He didn't say anything. I tried not to look at his face, but I couldn't help it. His face had shrunken and somehow the wrinkles had become like lines drawn sharply on clay. Looking at him made me feel sad. He opened his mouth to say something, but he soon closed it. I felt uneasy standing there before him. Suddenly he spoke.

'How is she?'

The question startled me.

'How is she? She? Oh, she's all right, Uncle.'

He stared at me, and I knew I had not answered his question satisfactorily.

'Did anyone see her give you this note?'

'Nobody saw her. She called me into their shop and gave it to me there.'

He nodded and seemed to relax. But he still made me

feel sad. There was a forced smile on his face. Then he put his hands on my head and fondled my hair.

'You know something?'

'No, Uncle.'

'You know we are partners in crime?'

I didn't know what he meant, so I said: 'No, Uncle.'

'What do you mean, "no"?'

'I mean, yes, Uncle.'

He stared at me, then he looked at the open note in his hand, and continued: 'How long have you been here with us, Keme?'

'I think it's been one month, Uncle.'

'Have you learned anything from us?'

I wondered why he was asking me all these questions, and stammered: 'Yes, Uncle.'

'Like what?'

I hesitated, then he urged: 'Go on.'

I said: 'How to cook, how to live with other people, how to take messages . . .'

'Eeemmm good,' he interrupted. 'Your father is wise in sending his children to live with relatives from time to time. It's good training. It makes them learn how to survive anywhere.'

He was looking above me. Then he brought out a bottle of whisky that was hidden under the chair and drank directly from it and quickly put it back. I knew he was hiding the bottle because of his wife. There would be a quarrel if she caught him drinking.

'Uncle, she said I should bring back a reply.'

He was not listening.

'Do you like my wife?' he asked suddenly.

I felt trapped. Uncle wasn't usually like that. He was either drunk or something. I did not know how to answer his question because I did not like his wife and I could not tell him so. She sent me about like a servant and knocked me on the head and gave me very small portions of food. But she was a beautiful woman and I liked looking at her.

'So you don't like my wife, eh?'

'I do, Uncle, I do.'

He looked down absent-mindedly at the note.

'Keme, do you know what I want most?'

He looked at me, his dark big eyes searching mine. I knew what Uncle Saba wanted most. That was one of the first things I learned when I came to the house. Whenever we went to church he prayed for it. Whenever he looked at me, he was praying for it. Every morning his wife would wake us up and we would all troop to the sitting-room and we all had to mention it in prayer. At first it puzzled me, but later it made me feel sorry for Uncle Saba.

'You want a child, Uncle,' I said.

He looked up at me slowly. It was ages before he spoke again.

'You know, God sometimes answers prayers the wrong way.'

I was surprised to hear him say that. He and his wife were good Christians. He tapped my head again.

'Keme, you know, I'm in trouble. But you're too young to know what kind of trouble.'

'Yes, Uncle.'

'Go and sleep. But keep everything to yourself, you understand?'

'Yes, Uncle.'

'Okay, you can go. What are you still waiting for?'

'She said I should bring back a reply.'

Uncle Saba looked even more tired.

He said: 'Don't worry. I will go and give it to her myself.'

'All right, Uncle,' I said, thinking about the ten kobo

she had promised me if I brought back a reply that night. But I did not need to worry. Uncle gave me thirty kobo instead. As I left the room I noticed that Uncle Saba had been looking over my head at the many pictures of his long marriage hanging on the walls behind me.

The next morning, after we had said prayers and Uncle's wife had gone to work, I went out to play. It was holiday time and there was little else to do. One thing I did not like about Uncle's area was that there weren't many children to play with. And the parents of those that were around did not like them playing when they could be working in the house. I decided to walk past Mary's shop. I was hoping that I might get some sweets from her and play with some of her little brothers.

'Keme!' a voice called. I stopped and turned. It wasn't Mary who had called; but I ran to the small shop where she sold provisions and vegetables. It was her brother who had called.

When I got there Mary stuck her head out of the shop and said: 'Come inside here.'

I went into the shop. I often wondered how she could live in that tiny space with her brothers and sisters. The place was choked with all sorts of baskets and boxes.

'Did you give Saba my letter, eh, Keme?'

'Yes, I gave it to him last night.'

'What about the reply?' she asked, shutting the door to make sure no one was listening.

I looked down at my slippers and my feet covered in dust.

'He said he would bring it himself.'

She sat back down in the dirty cane chair. I began to feel I shouldn't be there.

'What did he say exactly?'

I told her, but I exaggerated a little.

She looked at me seriously and said: 'You've been a

good boy. You've been doing this come-and-go messages for us. What does your madam say?'

'She doesn't know,' I assured her.

'True?'

'But sometimes she beats me if I stay out too long.'

'Is she a good woman?'

'I don't know.'

'But she hasn't given him a child yet.'

'We pray for it every day. One day it will come.'

Mary gave me a smile of amusement.

Then she asked: 'Will you like it if I marry him?'

I was surprised.

'Uncle Saba will not marry you. He's a Christian.'

She looked at me as if I had said something stupid.

Then she laughed quietly and said: 'What sort of Christian? Christian, eh? If you know the things we do together . . .'

I felt my face go hot that she was referring to Uncle in that way. I watched as the smile faded from her face. She was good-looking, her face lean and long, but her eyes were sad. She was tall and often wore shabby clothes and used a lot of eyeshadow and powder, but she was also slim in a nice way. I often wondered why Uncle sent so many messages to her and saw her secretly in the dark, especially when he had a wife who was better-looking and fatter. Maybe it was because Mary was kind, poor and not proud. When Mary spoke next it was with bitterness.

'Saba is avoiding me, eh? When we were doing it everything was sweet. Now that it has happened he doesn't want to see me again.'

'I want to go now,' I said.

'Okay. Tell Tommy to give you some sweets and come and play with them, you hear?'

I nodded and went outside. I thought I heard her

beginning to cry as soon as I closed the door. I went and played with her brothers and sisters. We played football and table tennis and they let me have a shower in their place. Then we went to watch a Chinese film together.

When I got home I was surprised to see Uncle's wife's car. She had finished early from work, or something had come up. I sneaked down the corridor to my room. They were talking loudly and I could not help listening.

'Darling, come on, let's go to the room.'

'I have a headache.'

'You've had this headache for over a week.'

'Hard work.'

'What kind of hard work?'

There was silence, then the sound of ruffled paper, then a restrained struggle, heavy breathing, and finally a sigh.

'Saba, do you have another woman, eh?'

'Why do you say such a stupid thing?'

'Then why are you behaving like this?'

'Look, I'm . . .'

'That's what you men say when it begins to happen.'

There was another long silence.

'Why did you come from work so early?'

'I went to the doctor's clinic.'

'What did he say? God has suddenly opened your womb?'

'You don't have to talk like that.'

Uncle didn't say anything for a while.

'We're getting old, you know,' he said after the pause.

'So what?'

'So what? So what, eh? It's as if you like being childless.'

'If it can't be helped, why grumble endlessly about it.'

'Because I want a child, that's why.'

'We've talked about this for over ten years now. I'm

tired. You know I've tried everything, but you just can't plant a baby.'

'I think I'll go and have a bath.'

Uncle's wife raised her voice when she said, sharply: 'If you want a baby that badly, then go and marry another wife. I know that's what you want.'

Uncle spoke tiredly and slowly.

'You know I don't want to marry another wife. You know my people have come here often and talked and got angry about that issue. You know that . . .'

I felt sorry for Uncle. I did not know why his voice failed and gave way to a sigh, but I suspected it was because of the trouble he told me that he was in.

'You see, you can't even finish, I know. I know that's why you've been having headaches and nose-aches and bedaches. But I swear, you will be in trouble if you do anything like that and I catch you.'

Then I heard a short wail and then a door slammed shut. As I stood there in the corridor I was worried that I'd heard something I shouldn't have. I was just about turning into my room when the door opened.

'Keme, what are you doing here? And where have you been all day? I've been looking for you.'

Uncle spoke softly. I felt guilty. Since I had come to the house I hadn't given him any cause to flog me. He liked me, in spite of the fact that his wife often said I stole meat from the pot when all I took once was a crayfish. I looked down.

Fondling my hair, Uncle Saba said: 'Your father sent a message. He wants you to come home for something. You shouldn't listen at doors to what people are saying, you hear?'

I nodded quickly and said: 'Yes, Uncle.'

He gave me a sharp little knock on the centre of my head that brought tears to my eyes.

'Go and pack your things,' he commanded.

'Am I going today?'

'No, you can go tomorrow.'

That evening they had another quarrel. I did not know what caused it, but it could have been the same thing as it was in the afternoon.

The next morning Uncle's wife did not ask us to the sitting-room to pray. Uncle Saba drove me to my father's house. I did not see his wife before I left and I was sure she did not care whether I came or went. During the drive Uncle was silent. I kept looking up at him and I knew he wanted to say something.

At a traffic jam he reached over and put his palm on my head and said: 'Keme, you enjoyed staying with us, didn't you?'

'Yes, Uncle, I enjoyed it.'

After a brief silence, he asked: 'Did you see Mary?'

'I saw her yesterday.'

'Did she say anything?'

'Yes. She said you are running away from her. That when you were doing it everything was sweet, and now that it has come you are running. Something like that . . .'

He took his hand from my head. I looked up at him. His face had darkened and his wrinkles had deepened. Suddenly he stepped on the brake. I was thrown forward and my forehead hit the dashboard. Uncle had just missed running over an old woman who had pursued her chicken into the main road.

'Are you all right?'

'A bit. It's only my head.'

'Foolish old woman. Wouldn't stay in bed. God forbid that I should kill an old woman.'

He didn't say anything more till we arrived at my father's house. When I was getting out of the car he gave me a small envelope containing two naira. I was overwhelmed.

'Thank you, Uncle.'

'It's all right, Keme,' he replied.

Then I said the only thing I could think of as a prayer: 'God will give you plenty of children, Uncle.'

He did not say 'Amen' several times as he used to when praying. His face only brightened and he got out of the car and put his hand on my shoulder and led me upstairs. In the next few weeks I did not hear much about Uncle and his wife and Mary.

My father had sent for me, it seemed, because of a traditional ceremony he wanted to perform. He always wanted his children present for such things. After I had resumed school, Uncle came to our house one evening carrying several things in his arms.

'Are you coming to stay with us, Uncle?' I asked.

He looked tired and lean and darker and older than when I had last seen him.

'No, Keme,' he replied.

Then I saw Mary climbing up the stairs behind him. I was quite speechless. What was Mary doing with Uncle in public? Then I saw her slightly protruding stomach.

Uncle seemed to be aware of the confusing things going on inside my head, for he whispered to me: 'Wait, I will tell you.'

Then they went into the sitting-room. My father was in his room serving his juju. I knocked on his back door and told him that Uncle Saba was here with a woman.

I am sure they must have discussed the visit before because when my father came out he said, smiling: 'Ah, so you've brought our little wife?'

Dad saw me standing at the corner of the room and his eyes hardened. I knew he wanted me to leave. I went to my room. They were in the sitting-room for a long time before Uncle came out. He knocked on my door and said he was going. I followed him downstairs to the car.

'Keme, you remember all those prayers?'

I nodded.

'Well, Mary is about to give me a child.'

'So she is going to be your wife, then?'

He smiled dryly.

'No, Keme.'

I did not say anything for a while, for I did not understand.

'Is this the trouble you said you were in the other day?'

'Yes. But it's not over yet. My wife does not know about this. So if you see her coming here, run inside and tell your father's wife, you hear?'

I nodded. It was becoming more and more difficult to understand.

Uncle continued: 'And try to help her in any way you can, eh? Like fetching water and things like that. I will be coming here from time to time.'

Then he patted my head, saying: 'I don't have any change now. I spent all my money buying things for when the baby arrives. So wait till I come next time, eh?'

I nodded again, but a bit reluctantly. When he got into the car I remembered what he said when I was staying with him.

So I said: 'Uncle, God has a strange way of answering prayers, not so?'

He smiled, started the engine, and answered: 'But then, God is strange.'

Uncle started to laugh. I didn't think I should join him. But maybe he was right.

Mary stayed with us through the dry season and into the rainy season. Her stomach grew bigger and bigger till it almost frightened me just to look at it. She was very hard-working and quiet. She helped my father's wife to cook and sometimes went to the market and often washed clothes. I came to like her very much. Her face became lean and she looked like one suffering.

Uncle seldom came. I thought it was wicked of him. He had a woman who was going to bear a child that he wanted so badly and he seldom came to see her. One day when we were in the sitting-room telling stories, we heard somebody running up and down the corridor, shouting. My father ran to the door. I was behind him. Then I saw Uncle's wife.

She carried a machete and shouted wildly: 'Let me see that prostitute who is going to deliver a bastard! Let me fling off her neck, the smelling rat, stinking prostitute . . .'

It was difficult to believe what was happening. She bellowed and screamed that she would kill Mary and kill herself. My father talked to her and quietened her, but it took more than five people to restrain her rage. Later, she was driven home by Dad. Mary was disturbed. I felt sorry for her and the child. Still Uncle never came.

We heard later that Uncle had not come because whenever he wanted to go out, his wife would say: 'Ah, so you're sneaking out to meet that prostitute again?'

And so Uncle never came just to please her. He didn't come even when Mary had her baby. It was a boy, strong and big, and it resembled his father. I was happy and did not feel sad any more.

Another two weeks passed before Uncle turned up and he was surprised that Mary had delivered. We were all angry with him. But he was happy and he smiled a lot and he didn't mind the things we said.

A few weeks later Uncle came and said he had rented a place for her. It was a tiny room on the street next to ours. We thought that maybe Uncle was at last coming to his senses and his responsibilities. But even when Mary moved, Uncle still seldom came to see her. It was my

father who gave her money to buy food and later she
opened a small provisions stall.

Then we heard that Uncle's wife had left him. She had
gone to court and obtained a divorce. In the meantime,
Uncle had lost his job; because of all the troubles he
hadn't been working properly.

The next time I saw him I was shocked. He was like a
man who had just come out of prison. I did not feel sorry
for him any more. We felt he had brought it on himself.
He came with drinks to ask my father to forgive him for
not coming all along. He was a different person.

'Keme,' he said to me, 'you see what life can do to a
man?'

'You've changed, Uncle,' I said.

'I have been suffering,' he answered.

He was ashamed to look at me. His eyes had gone
inside. He hadn't shaved for many days.

'My wife has taken all my things,' he sobbed.

'How manage?'

'The court gave it to her.'

'The court is stupid.'

'No, it's me who has been stupid.'

I remained silent, and after a while Uncle said: 'She is
now going around with another man, a rich man in her
working-place.'

My father, who hadn't spoken much, cut in and said:
'When God gives you a blessing, take it.'

I said: 'But God is a funny person.'

My father said: 'Shut up, Keme. God is not funny.'

Uncle said: 'God is making life unbearable for me.'

My father gave me money to go and buy myself some
sweets. I knew it was a way of getting me to leave them
alone. Later, I followed Uncle Saba to Mary's place. She
was cooking rice and beans when we got there. The baby
was sleeping and tied to her back with a wrapper.

Her face darkened when she saw Uncle. She was angry and she raised both her fists and rushed at him. But when she got there she threw her arms round his neck. Uncle smiled. We went inside the room. It was airless and tight. I could see Mary was making the best of things. She had bought herself a centre table and some chairs and a small electric fan.

She brought Uncle some beer and brought me a Coke. The baby woke up and began crying. Mary took him off her back, carried him in her arms, and hushed him. Uncle, who began fidgeting uneasily, wanted to carry him. The baby looked wide-eyed at Uncle and, as though suspicious, began crying.

'Sssshhh,' I said. The baby hushed.

'Do you know who this ugly man is?' Mary asked the baby, playfully.

The baby looked wide-eyed at Uncle again.

'He's your father,' I said.

The baby gave us a toothless and radiant grin. We all felt happy. After that Uncle came and lived with Mary in that small room. In a way, I think Uncle was right when he said that God was strange.

The Dream-vendor's August

AJEGUNLE JOE SPENT the evening reading the letters from the few subscribers he had left. Without a single exception they called him a fraud and demanded back their money. When he had finished reading he was very depressed. He went to a bar and got quite drunk, but that didn't improve anything. So he went to his favourite hotel to look for a cheap prostitute. That didn't help either. He kept hearing the subscribers in his head. In the end he paid the woman for her time and left more depressed than he had arrived. He got home, lit two mosquito coils, and climbed into bed. He forgot to lock the door. Soon he was snoring.

He dreamt about a woman with a rugged face and indifferent eyes. All through the dream he didn't have an erection. When he woke up it was with the certainty that someone had been in the room while he was asleep. He saw the open door and soon found that large quantities of printing paper, his tubes of printing ink, his transistor radio, his pornographic magazines, and a book he much valued called *The Ten Wonders of Africa*, were missing.

He sat on the bed. He stared at the almanacs of

long-bearded mystics on the wall. Somewhere in him was the feeling that a pain he had lived with had suddenly edged towards the unbearable. He had the taste of tangerines in his mouth. He was two weeks into the month of August.

When July passed with its thunderous downpours, and when August advanced with its dry winds and browning elephant grass, Joe felt himself at the mercy of a cyclical helplessness. Two years earlier, around the same time, Joe lost a woman he had been planning to marry. They had met one day to discuss their future together. Joe had catarrah. He made the mistake of blowing his nose in her presence, the act of which produced a long and disgusting sound. She didn't show her disapproval, but afterwards all talk of marriage was avoided. When later on he learnt that she had become engaged to another man, Joe was shattered. He went around in a daze. He no longer walked with his former arrogant swing. He became clumsy and unsure of himself. He lost his job. One night in a bar when he tried to sound like his former arrogant self, he got involved in a fight and had two of his front teeth knocked into his mouth. Then he took to strangling his laughter.

It was after the woman left his life, after his birthday in September, that he got another job in a small printing press. He took Correspondence Courses in psychology and salesmanship and earned himself two diplomas. He developed an unusual interest in the occult and in mysticism. His thoughts became too deep for him and his dreams became more mysterious. He gradually experienced himself being taken over by a new personality. He took to writing down his visions and dreams: then he began publishing them as cheap pamphlets. The first pamphlet was called *Mysteries of Orumaka*. Quite a few people bought it and he was encouraged by the modest sales. With the help of his boss he printed pamphlets like: *How to Sleep Soundly*, *How to Have Powerful Dreams*, *How to Fight Witches and Wizards*, and *How to Banish Poverty from Your Life*. The pamphlets achieved some limited popularity but they didn't make him any money. Sometimes when there wasn't much work at the printing press Ajegunle Joe would take bundles of his pamphlets to sell on the molue buses. It was in the Christmas of that year that it occurred to him to set up a Correspondence Course on how people could improve their lives. He discussed it with his boss and they agreed to split profits. Two adverts were placed in the newspapers and soon they had subscribers. The Correspondence Course was named: 'Turn Life into Money'.

And then came the following August. Tax inspectors took a sudden interest in him. His mother fell ill and he had to go home and see her. When he got back the landlord had taken it into his head to increase the rent. It was an August of elections, political fevers and riggings. Ajegunle Joe's dreams became so violent that he wrote and printed a treasonable tract called: *The Farce Which Will Become History*. Nobody bought the tract and one night the printer's shop was raided by soldiers, who carried away all existing copies. The police got hold of Joe the next day, and he was jailed for two weeks without any charges being brought against him. Then, suddenly, he was released. He wrote to all the newspapers about his arrest, but because no one knew him, and everyone was afraid, his letters were never published. What made matters worse was that his boss suddenly opted out of their joint venture, deducted half the losses from Joe's salary, and then gave him the sack. But what saved Joe was that the new personality had taken him over completely. He spent the rest of the year selling his pamphlets in the day and occasionally working at the docks in the night.

This August was no better. Business had been worse than usual. Printing paper was scarce. And he felt stale. Nothing moved in him that morning. He found himself at the point where his faith in his own Correspondence Course had reached its lowest.

He got up from the bed and opened the window. He went to the toilet and then had a shower. Back in his room he lit a stick of incense. He fetched a tumbler of water, breathed deeply, and drank, facing the east. He sat in one of his chairs. He intoned some vowel sounds and then he meditated on an empty stomach. By the time he had finished meditating and sealing his morning prayers with occultic signs, he had begun to accept the reality of his losses. He made some food and ate. He was about to start cleaning his room when he heard someone calling to him from outside.

'Is Jungle Joe in? Jungle Joe! Your friend is here.'

His friend, Cata-cata, knocked and came into the room. They called him by that name because he used to be a hard-headed generator of confusion. He had quietened down now; he was even thinking of marriage. He used to be a boxer, but after being knocked out in the first round of an unmemorable featherweight match, he seemed to settle for the anonymity of being a lady's man. He was tall and solemn; he had a wide nose and narrow eyes. He wore a Ghanian print shirt and khaki trousers. He worked regular night-shifts at the docks. In the day-time he fished. He smiled broadly at Joe when he came into the room. He had two mangoes in his hand. He had a Ghanian woman with him. She was robust, and her body was slow in its thick sweaty sensuality. She had fleshy lips, a kind face, and she smiled a lot. She carried an orange and two bottles of small stout.

'How are you Joe?' Cata-cata said, slapping his friend on the back.

'Not too good.'

'Why, what's happened?'

'Everything.'

'Have you met my friend?' Cata-cata said to the Ghanian woman. She was still smiling.

'Well, this is Ajegunle Joe, occultist and dreamer. Joe, this is my girlfriend, Sarah.'

They greeted one another. The Ghanian woman avoided meeting Joe's eyes. They were all still standing. Cata-cata offered Joe a mango.

'No, thank you, my friend. Things are so bad I don't have a mouth for fruits,' Joe said.

'That's a shame.'

'Cata-cata, I've just been robbed.'

'When?' Cata-cata said, taking a seat and indicating to Sarah that she do the same. She sat on the bed.

'Today. When I was asleep.'

'You mean they robbed you when you were asleep?'

'Yes,' said Joe, dryly.

'What sort of sleep is that? You must have been drinking too much.'

Cata-cata laughed in the direction of the woman.

'I think I left the door open,' said Joe unsmilingly.

'What did they take?'

'Pamphlets. Clothes. They took the transistor radio and . . .'

'That radio?' interrupted Cata-cata, laughing again in the direction of the woman.

'They must have been desperate . . .'

'And worst of all,' said Joe, 'they took that book that I got. *The Ten Wonders of Africa*.'

'I'm sorry to hear that,' said Cata-cata with laughter still on his face.

Ajegunle Joe nodded. He was feeling in bad humour. He sat on a stool and kept eyeing the woman. Looks very ripe, he thought. Then he felt bitter that for two years he had been without a regular woman.

'I can't offer you drinks,' Joe said suddenly.

'What is drinks between friends, eh? Besides, we brought our own.'

The Ghanian woman crossed her legs. Then she put the bottles of stout on the table. There was a long silence. There was some embarrassment in the air. Cata-cata kept trying to catch Joe's eyes.

'So how is the course doing?'

'Bad,' said Joe, staring grimly at his friend. Cata-cata made signs for Joe to leave the room. Joe pretended not to notice. He continued with what he was saying.

'One of my subscribers ran into trouble,' he said in an even voice.

'How?'

'She followed my instructions and got sacked. She wants her money back.'

'What instructions?' Cata-cata said, gesticulating furiously.

'In the first lesson I instructed them to look fearlessly at people in the eye and to speak up forcefully. Well, her boss didn't like it when she did.'

Cata-cata laughed again. The Ghanian woman laughed as well. She looked very youthful when she laughed and her breasts rocked. Joe remained dour.

When the general laughter had subsided Cata-cata said, with more intentionality than was needed: 'Joe, aren't you going out? It's going to rain soon, you know.'

'It's not supposed to rain in August.'

'But it's going to rain, anyway,' Cata-cata said, glaring at Joe.

'So why should I go out if it's going to rain soon, eh?'

He knew Cata-cata was referring to their usual arrangement. I've been robbed, Joe thought, and all my friend can think about is sex.

'Because you can go out and come back before it rains, that's why.'

'I see,' said Joe.

Cata-cata, surprised at his friend's incomprehension, looked from Joe to the woman and back again.

'You know what I mean,' he said, with some desperation.

'I don't know,' Joe replied, sweating in pretended ignorance. 'How can I know when I've been robbed, eh? And all the subscribers want their money back. I don't know anything, my friend.'

Joe was very serious. Look at all that is happening to me, he thought, and all he wants to do is make love to this woman in my room.

'By the way,' Joe said aloud, 'what is wrong with your room, eh?'

Cata-cata was alarmed. He stammered. He had a regular girlfriend; she had a key to his room; and she made it a habit to turn up at the oddest hours. There was even talk of marriage between them. He wanted the Ghanian woman quickly, on the side. He couldn't risk the use of his own room, and Joe knew this well.

'I have a relative staying,' Cata-cata said, almost pleadingly.

Ajegunle Joe stared at him unsympathetically. Cata-cata suddenly stood up.

'I want to talk to you outside,' he said to Joe.

They both went out.

'You're a bastard!' Cata-cata said, the moment they were outside.

'Things are hard,' Joe said.

'What are you trying to do? Spoil my fun, eh?'

'Things are bad.'

'So what? Aren't we friends? Look. Relax. We'll go fishing later.'

'What will that do for me?'

'You might catch a fish. You've never caught a fish.'

'A fish won't pay my rent. A fish won't get those thieves.'

'You are mad.'

'All of us are mad.'

'Rubbish.'

They were silent for a moment. They could see the back of the Ghanian woman through the window. She fidgeted. She played with the orange.

'You know she likes you.'

'Who?'

'Sarah. I've done a build-up of you. I can tell she likes you. Have her afterwards. She won't mind.'

'How do you know?'

'What do you mean? She is a good, fun-loving woman.'

'I don't want her afterwards,' Joe said, looking at her back through the window.

'What do you want then, eh?'

'Money.'

'Money?'

'Lend me some money.'

'More? You owe me ten already.'

'Give me another ten.'

'I am not a bank.'

'Give me ten. I'll sell some pamphlets today. I'll pay you back when some subscriptions come in.'

'And when will that be?'

'Today, tomorrow, soon.'

'You've been saying that for two years now.'

'Lend me ten.'

'Okay.'

'Things are hard.'

'Things are always hard for you.'

'They'll get better.'

'When do you want it?'

'Now.'

'Now?'

'Yes.'

Cata-cata gave Joe the ten naira. They went back in without exchanging another word.

The Ghanian woman had started peeling the orange with her fingers when they both came in. Cata-cata sat down on the bed next to her. He put his arm round her.

Joe said: 'I'm going to check my post office box before it rains. Do you want some stamps?'

'No.'

Ajegunle Joe looked at the woman as she ate the orange. With her palm she wiped the juice that flowed down the sides of her mouth.

Struck by the fleshiness of her thighs, noticing the succulence of her lips, Joe said: 'Have you read any of my pamphlets?'

'No,' said the woman.

'You should. There are many powers in this world.'

'Leave her alone,' Cata-cata said, caressing her neck.

'They call me the Dream-vendor,' Joe said, 'because I am at the mercy of my dreams. I am the man who runs the Cosmic Power Correspondence Course. Have you ever heard of it?'

'Leave her alone,' Cata-cata said. 'She can't read and

she doesn't have any money to subscribe. Leave the poor girl alone.'

'Yes, I have,' the woman said.

Both men turned towards her.

'My younger brother is taking your course. He thinks it's all right. Every morning he looks into the mirror and says strange things. He drinks a glass of water, breathes deeply and starts making funny noises. He is always asking me the direction of the east. He is going to university in Ghana next year. He always smells of bad incense.'

Ajegunle Joe was surprised. He beamed. He held up his head. He was so amazed that he didn't say anything. His throat kept moving. His mood immediately improved and he wore his battered galoshes and the greatcoat he had bought cheaply from amongst the stolen goods at the docks. He bustled around the room. He moved with a forced swing that tossed the bulk of the coat one way and another. The swagger suited him fine.

He said: 'People need advice. People need power. To see far is the only way to win the battles of this terrible life.'

The Ghanian woman said: 'My brother takes several other courses. About five of them. Every night he does a different thing. Sometimes he mixes up all the instructions. He is too serious. I think he is going mad.'

She had finished eating the orange. Her eyes shone brilliantly. She stopped smiling.

Ajegunle Joe didn't seem to have heard what she said, because he went on to deck himself out with his talismanic necklaces. He made a show of wearing his three rings. He explained their powers as he wore them. One of them was called 'The Ring of Merlin'. It was supposed to have been brought to Africa by Portuguese sailors. It had the magic number 7 in green; it was guaranteed to make him invisible in time of danger. Then there was 'The Ring of Master Eckhart'. He was a German mystic. This ring, Joe said, had been additionally treated by a Spanish divine. The third one, with its red triangle, was 'The Ring of Aladdin'. It had been found on the dead body of Isaac Newton.

'For every act there is an equal and opposite reaction,' Joe said. He winked at his friend. He bared the gap in his front teeth in a smile to the woman.

He said: 'Nothing stays still. Do it gently, but think of my poor bed.'

He swung the back of his coat and made for the door. Soon he had the sky opening above him.

He paused just outside his room. He stood still, listening. He heard the bed creak.

He heard Cata-cata say: *'What are you waiting for?'*

Then the window was slammed shut.

Joe went up the street, towards the main road. The air was dense and unpleasant with the smell of the evaporating gutters. It was August and the bushes near uncompleted houses were thickly filmed with dust, and no trees were in bloom.

The main road was cluttered with multiple traffic jams. Drivers sweated at the steering wheels: they looked as if they were undergoing the most perverse of punishments. Joe felt a peculiar freedom walking past the vehicles in the standstill, so he began to stride. In the second lesson of his Correspondence Course, Joe says: 'The way you carry yourself is the way you want people to think of you.' When Joe cuts down the road he looks like an amiable scarecrow. He walks too stylishly. People sometimes say that too much style betrays hunger.

There was chaos at the post office. Queues stretched out from the building and down the road. Joe checked his box: there weren't any subscriptions, but there were enquiries about his catalogue. He joined the end of the queue and it was a while before he got anywhere near the counter. He heard someone in the queue saying that the post office workers were so underpaid that they were now sabotaging the post. When he got to the counter it took some time, and some shouting, before any of the clerks paid him any attention.

The clerk said: 'Why are you shouting as if you are in your mother's kitchen?'

'God punish you for saying that,' Joe said.

An argument ensued and Joe got so worked up he felt his heart hammering unnaturally against his ribs. He quietened down. The clerk went on abusing him. Joe suffered the abuses in silence. He bought his stamps. He was counting his change when he suddenly felt a searing sensation in his crotch. He pushed his way out through the crowd; but the crowd pushed back on him. He found himself being squashed to the metallic frame of the door and he was overcome with panic. He started shouting, swearing, fighting his way out.

He was on his way back home when the sky came closer to the ground. Petty traders and stall-owners rushed to clear their goods. Joe continued to stride on stylishly. There was commotion everywhere. Thunder exploded overhead. The road was lit in a moment's incandescence. The sky darkened and lightning split the air. The rain pelted down in a hurry. Gutters began to overflow and vehicles, avoiding the potholes, splashed mud all over Ajegunle Joe's greatcoat. He was soon thoroughly drenched and he had to run all the way home with water squelching in his galoshes.

Cata-cata and the woman had gone when Joe got back. Water ran down his back, along his spine. He shivered. He found the key under the doormat.

It was hot in the room. Joe undressed, dried himself, and wore fresh clothes all through the sex smells of the heated room. He couldn't open the window; the rain would come in. So he lit a stick of incense.

Cata-cata and the Ghanian woman had left the orange peelings and the mango seeds on the centre table. The two bottles of stout were empty. The bed was very rough. Flies had come into the room. Joe became very despondent. He changed the sheets and climbed into bed. He slept through the steady drone of the falling rain. He dreamt that the rain had been falling for a long time and the great voice of thunder spoke intermittently from the sky. People were wailing and there was a beautiful music pervading the world. He felt he knew the music, though he had never heard it before.

And then a midget with a large head and red eyes came to him and said: 'How are you?'

'Fine,' Joe said.

'Good.'

'How long has it been raining?' Joe asked the midget.

'Forty days.'

Joe stared at the midget. The music stopped, the rain increased.

The midget said: 'Open your eyes.'

'They are open,' Joe said.

'No they're not. Open them.'

Joe opened his eyes and woke up. The rain was heavier and water had been flowing into his room from beneath the door. Joe stayed in bed. He turned over and listened to his stomach rumbling. He fell back asleep and the midget came to him again.

'I told you your eyes were shut,' the midget said.

'You did.'

'How can you see me if they are shut?'

'Faith,' said Joe.

The midget laughed.

'I like you,' the midget said.

'I don't know you,' Joe said, 'but I like you too.'

'You talk in riddles.'

'I'm sorry,' said Joe.

'I hate people who are sorry,' the midget said.

'But you just said you liked me.'

'I do. That's why I'm going to give you something. But when I come and ask for it, you must give it back.'

'That's fine,' said Joe.

The midget put something in Joe's palm and closed the fingers over it. Joe opened his hand and a blue light flashed in his eyes, but Joe didn't see anything.

'You didn't give me anything,' Joe said.

'Yes I did. But it's flown away now. I didn't ask you to look at it, did I?'

'What was it?' Joe asked.

'Wisdom.'

Joe was quiet for a moment.

'Why don't you give me something else then?'

The midget gave him something and told him to put it away. Joe put it in his pocket. The midget grinned and then disappeared.

When Joe woke up it had stopped raining. He spent some of the evening looking at his finances, which were very low. Then he tried to do some more work on the fifteenth lesson of his Correspondence Course. He had been writing on the theme of adversity and he couldn't find anything more to say on the subject. All he had written was: 'Adversity is the secret way to the centre, to the base and springboard. Train your muscles before you leap. Train your head before you soar.' The pile of manuscript lay beside him on the bed. He tried to think about adversity, but he succeeded only in thinking about women. He thought about sex, without getting hot. He soon fell back asleep.

Ajegunle Joe spent the morning sweeping the water out from his room. Centipedes and worms had come in with the water. He caught the worms, to use sometime for fishing, and put them in a bottle. In the afternoon he took large quantities of his pamphlets and went out. At the main road bus conductors shouted their destination and there was commotion as people rushed to embark. Joe was astonished to find that a bus stop had materialized at the top of his street. With the bus stop had also come Ogogoro retailers, corn-roasters, petty traders, prostitutes, pickpockets. Ajegunle Joe bought himself a tumbler of Ogogoro and drank it slowly. He surveyed the bickering crowd, unable to believe his luck. When he finished the Ogogoro he began selling his pamphlets. In three hours he made thirty naira, selling off the pamphlets he brought with him. He went home and fetched some more; but by the time he got back most of the crowd had gone.

In the evening Joe went to a bar near his place for a quiet celebratory drink. He had been drinking heavily for a while, turning words and phrases on adversity in his head, when he noticed a woman sitting alone at a corner table. She looked familiar. Her face was bruised and puffed under the eyes. She had a plaster on her forehead, bandages on her left arm, and a wound just above her left ankle. She wore a black dress and white high-heeled shoes. Every time Joe dropped his tumbler and looked in her direction he was convinced she had just looked away. This went on till Joe eventually caught her eye. It was the Ghanian woman. She stared at him totally without recognition. He ordered two small bottles of stout, picked up his drink, and went over to join her.

'What happened to you?'

'None of ya business.'

'Aren't you Sarah, Cata-cata's woman?'

'Don't talk to me.'

'Don't you remember me?'

'Eh, so what?'

'What have I done to you, eh?'

'Birds of a feather . . .'

'What feather?'

'. . . shit together.'

'Hah! Sarah! What is this, eh?'

She stared stubbornly through him. He got up and opened one of the bottles of stout at the counter. When he got back she was smiling. She looked almost ghoulish with her puffed eyes, and her deranged, upturned lips.

'So how are you?' Joe asked.

'Shut up and pour me some of the stout,' she said.

'Sarah! Take it easy.'

'You men are like paper.'

He poured out her drink. She finished the tumbler of stout in a single gulp. She took out a cigarette and lit it. She stared at him.

'Talk to me,' she said, with glinting eyes.

Joe couldn't think of anything to say. After she had finished the two bottles of stout Joe went and got her three more.

'I can't finish three,' she said.

Joe stared at the ring she had on her middle finger. It was a large red ring with the white face of a little tiger.

'What sort of ring is that, eh?'

'Protection,' she said.

'What sort of protection?'

'From stupid men like ya friend,' she said.

'Sarah, tell me what happened. Did you quarrel?'

She played with her ring. She drank down another bottle, wiped her mouth, and then she went to the toilet.

When she came back she told him what had happened. After she and Cata-cata had finished in Joe's room they went to the bus stop. Cata-cata was seeing her off home when suddenly a woman stepped out from the crowd and blocked their path. The woman turned out to be Cata-cata's regular girlfriend.

'You should have seen her. She was just like a witch,' Sarah said.

'And what happened?'

'What do you think happened? She started shouting. Cursing. Screaming. And you should have seen Cata-cata. He's big for nothing. He was begging her. Begging her. In public. And then he began to lie about me to my own very face. He said I was just a friend. And then he said I was your new girlfriend. He denied me to my own face.'

'Then what happened?'

'His girlfriend scratched his face and spat in his eyes. The next thing was that both of them were fighting. In public. She picked up a stick and knocked him on the head. He slapped her. You should have heard her scream. Just like a witch. Quickly she ran and picked up a stone. He grabbed her and slapped her again. She dropped the stone and threw sand in his eyes. He went mad. He started hitting everywhere and he slapped me and then I too joined the fight. I joined her. Both of us jumped on him and he beat us and then a soldier came with a whip and flogged us and we ran. That friend of yours is a coward. He and his woman went home and settled their quarrel.'

Joe stared at her incredulously. He went and bought two bottles of beer for himself. He drank while staring at her. She didn't seem to notice his gaze.

'Cata-cata is my best friend, but I'm not like that. Big people don't need courage. I protect my friends.'

'Shit,' she said.

'I can help you,' he said solemnly.

'Help yourself.'

They fell silent.

Then Sarah said: 'Why do you men like thin girls with big breasts, eh?'

Joe thought for a long time before he said: 'I like girls like you.'

She stared at him from reddened eyes. She stood up.

'Where are you going now?'

She picked up the two remaining bottles of stout.

Then she said: 'Men are always asking stupid questions.'

They went out together.

He had hardly shut the window and locked the door when he felt her kissing his neck. He felt the full softness of her wet lips. He felt hot, but he didn't feel right. He felt very hot, a great yearning ached in him, he began to tremble. She kissed his face over and he noticed that she had a freckled tongue. He reached down under her pants and he was blasted by the surprising texture of her pubic hair. She was richly wet. He took off her clothes and saw that she had beads round her waist. He spent a long time kissing her breasts and playing with the circlets of hair round her nipples. Her breasts quivered. He took off his magic rings and his clothes and they went to bed. She was hot and her eyes were heavy-lidded. She still had her strange ring on. She struck him as one of those fortunate women who feel deeply their own arousal and whom it takes little touches to satisfy. He didn't like the women who were remote from their own desires, whom he would make love to from sunrise to sundown with them still seeking their elusive climaxes.

He fingered her and kissed her. He went up her, but it wasn't right. He couldn't understand. She was wet and willing, half-sunken in euphoria, waiting, it seemed, for a mere full penetration, but he wasn't hard. So he tried. He tried to dissolve himself into her desire, to feel the spell-breaking reality of her nakedness. He breathed in her potent, shameless body smells. And she waited. And he tried.

Then eventually he said: 'I think something is wrong.'

'What?'

'I don't know.'

'You don't want to do it?'

'I want to do it wickedly, but . . . it's not hard.'

She played with his private part desultorily, impatiently, wrenching it to both sides, dragging it down, talking gruffly to it, but still nothing came of her efforts. Suddenly she got out of bed. She dressed furiously.

'You and ya friend are completely useless,' she said.

Ajegunle Joe started to apologize, to suggest alternatives, but she slapped him hard on the face. Before he could recover she had gone out into the August night, leaving behind her two unopened bottles of stout.

Ajegunle Joe stared at the door. He sat on the bed. Then he got dressed. He wore his red, long-billed cap. He went out and bought himself a large tumbler of Ogogoro. He spent the evening staring at the almanacs of the long-bearded mystics, without seeing them. He fell asleep with the red cap still on his head.

Joe spent the next two days in misery. He went to a petty chemist and bought an ointment for gonorrhoea and tablets for 'increased virility'. They were expensive. They did not solve his problem. And his problem did not help the sales of his pamphlets. On the third day when he got up to do his improvised sales talk on the molue buses, his mouth was dry, his voice was thin and unconvincing, and people laughed at him. He also found, to his chagrin, that he had serious competitors. Some of them sold pamphlets foretelling the future, complete guides to palm-reading, even pamphlets that professed herbal cures for everything from leprosy to rheumatism. Humiliated, carried away by the intensity of competition, Joe began to denounce the regime, the society, policemen, soldiers. He made predictions of violent riots in the north, and tribal cannibalism in the south. It was unfortunate for him, however, that there were two policemen in mufti on the bus. But it was fortunate for him that he was only thrown off: he would otherwise most certainly have spent the rest of August in prison. Joe was not particularly bothered by the man-handling: the policemen were northerners; besides, he always believed that when people didn't like a dream he offered, it was usually because the dream was true.

After Joe had been thrown off the molue bus he headed homewards. He was wearing his red, long-billed cap, a jacket too large at the shoulders, his three talismanic rings, a shabby pair of blue trousers, and his galoshes. He was an unhappy sight. He went past a mechanic's workshop and a herbalist's signboard. Next to the board there was a red-painted shed. The door of the shed opened slowly as Ajegunle Joe went past. Then a chicken with a red cloth tied to its foot came out, and then went back into the shed. Joe should have remembered the fourteenth lesson of his own Correspondence Course, which says: 'Every human being has got something to be afraid of, in the form of signs.' But Joe didn't remember. Without thinking, he sneaked into the shed.

It was dark inside. He smelt animal blood, stale palm wine, and excellent cooking. When his eyes got used to the darkness he saw shelves on which were candles, bones, bundles of spiders' webs, jars, bottles, snake-skins. Something brushed against his galoshes and he screamed, jumping backwards. It was a turtle. Then he saw the numerous snails on the walls. A lizard regarded him from a niche.

'Is anybody in?'

He heard a cough. Then he noticed the other room in the shed, partioned by an antelope screen. Someone was in the room, in the half-light, eating. Joe smelt smoked-shrimps, fried plantain, bush meat, and he salivated.

'Who is there?' he said.

The chicken went out of the room, past the partition. A door opened. He heard water being poured into a glass.

The lights came on suddenly and then a voice said: 'The minute I saw your red cap I knew you were mine! Come in. Sit down. My name is Aringo. I am the most underrated herbalist in this God-forsaken city.'

Joe went into the inner room.

'So. Yes. What do you want? You have family problems? A strange illness? Is someone stealing your job from you? You have woman problems? Sit down! If you have money, I can cure anything.'

Joe sat on a stool. The herbalist stared at him expectantly. He had a bony, rugged face, and blazing eyes. He sweated gloriously. He wore a red soutane and he had beads round his neck. He had a long tongue which kept showing when he spoke.

'Talk! Talk! What's your problem? Have you come just to look at me? That cost's money, you know,' the herbalist said, baring his yellow teeth.

Joe was stuck for words.

The herbalist, increasing the volume of his voice, said: 'Look, mister man, I don't have time to stare at you. Can't you speak, eh? Have you got mosquitoes in your brain, eh?'

Joe still couldn't find anything to say. He stammered beneath his breath.

'Did someone beat you up, eh? I can give you medicine for fighting. You will be able to fight three men for seven days non-stop and you won't even be tired. You won't even sweat. That medicine costs ten naira, but it's guaranteed.'

Joe's continued silence began to exasperate the herbalist, who stood up suddenly. He strode up and down the inner room with the quick, angular movements of a cricket. That was when Joe noticed the figure of a warrior juju in a dark corner of the room. It was covered in candle wax, bits of kola nuts, native chalk, feathers of birds. It glistened with libations.

It looked very menacing, very attentive, standing there in the dark.

The herbalist said: 'Get up. Come and see this.'

The herbalist took the cover off a clay pot. Joe got up and went over. Something large and red pumped at the bottom of the pot.

'This is a crocodile's heart. Come and look at this.'

He showed Joe an earthenware pot: there was a snake curled up in its transparent liquid.

'Now. Tell me your problem and I will help you.'

It took some time before Joe managed to say, in a whisper: 'It's woman problem.'

'Ah-*hah*! So it's *woman problem*, eh?'

'Yes.'

'What kind of woman problem? You don't have a woman, or is there one in particular . . .'

'I tried to do it but I couldn't do it,' Joe said, hurriedly.

'What couldn't you do? Tell me. Don't be afraid.'

'It wouldn't stand up.'

'You mean you had a woman there, naked, and it wouldn't stand up?'

'Yes,' Joe said in a whisper.

'I didn't hear you.'

'Yes.'

'You should have said so. It's a small problem. Is that all you were whispering to me? Is that what you are ashamed of, eh?'

'Yes.'

'Do you think you are the first person to suffer it?'

'No.'

'The English people have a name for it. They call it *impotence*.'

'I know.'

'So you know? I see.'

He gave Joe a severe look.

'Take down your trousers,' the herbalist suddenly commanded.

'*What?*'

'I said take down your trousers. Let me see what's wrong with you.'

'But . . .'

'But what? What's wrong with you, eh? You think you are special, eh? This month alone I have circumcised two white men. I have treated three Lebanese men for gonorrhoea. Not to mention the Portuguese women. So you think you are special, eh? Okay. Go! Leave my shed! Get out and carry your *impotence* with you!'

Joe coyly lowered his trousers and his underpants. The herbalist inspected him.

'Is it this tiny thing you're ashamed of, eh?'

Joe was silent. The herbalist continued with his inspection and then said: 'You are lucky. You don't have gonorrhoea.'

He straightened. Joe pulled up his trousers. He looked defeated.

The herbalist said: 'How much have you got?'

Joe stammered. The herbalist did not press the point.

He said: 'In this my shed I have everything you need. I can give you the sexual power of a horse, or of a hippopotamus. They cost differently, of course. Talk to me. What do you want to fuck like? A tiger? A lion? You want to do it like a cat, or quickly like a dog? I have different things for women, too. If you both want to be powerful in bed, all it takes is money.'

'If I want to do it like a bull, how much will that cost?' Joe risked asking.

The herbalist eyed him disdainfully.

He said: 'You won't be able to afford that one. I sold that medicine to a Portuguese man last month. He came back three times for more. So. Which one do you want?'

There was another silence.

'Will the medicine work immediately?'

'Yes. Guaranteed.'

Another silence.

Then the herbalist suddenly, sharply, said: 'Take off those rings! Take them off!'

Joe started.

'Take them off! *Now!* Unless you have come here to *challenge* me.'

Joe still didn't understand what was happening. The herbalist bent over and pulled off his red soutane. His chest and stomach were covered in weird scarifications. He had a bulbous navel.

'If you want my treatment, take off those rings,' the herbalist said, reaching for a cutlass, which he waved menacingly in the air.

Joe took off the rings and put them in his coat pocket. The herbalist still waved the cutlass as if he might use it.

He said: 'They are useless rings. Quack rings. I have got better ones. I have got one that shows you if you are healthy and it flashes before there is danger. I have got a ring that will make any woman you want come to you. I have got another one that you wear only when you are discussing a lot of money. That one costs a lot. I have even got one of King Solomon's rings. I won't sell it. So. Which one do you want, eh?'

'I'll have the medicine of an antelope,' Joe said eventually.

The herbalist was relieved.

'It costs thirty naira. Not a kobo more, not a kobo less.'

Joe had only thirty-five naira on him.

'Okay,' he said, weakly.

His course of treatment consisted of having to wash in murky herbal water, rubbing the afflicted part with a dark, grainy ointment, and drinking a tasteless pot of soup in which had been supposedly sprinkled the grindings of an antelope's testicles. Then a fire was built in the backyard which he had to extinguish with his urine. When he finished the course of treatment nothing happened. Joe gave it some time and then he got angry and demanded his money back; but people were knocking on the outside door.

The herbalist, having already lost interest in him, said: 'Be patient. Go home and be patient. I've got other customers at the door.'

'You are a crook. You are a thief,' Joe shouted.

The herbalist's face darkened, his nose flared; but he went to a niche, came back, and gave Joe his business card.

'Go home. If by Saturday nothing happens, come and burn down my shed.'

Joe took the card and stamped out of the shed. He felt nauseous, cheated, and foolish.

Joe caught a bus home.

He got a seat at the back, near the window. The traffic moved slowly. The road and pavement were full of trinket sellers, hawkers of smoked fish, petty traders of bread and boiled eggs. Without being aware of it, Joe had been watching a girl who sold oranges. Now and again the girl broke out and sang: 'Sweet orange re-o!' She had a clear, beautiful voice.

It wasn't long before Joe became aware that he had been staring at her. She had browned teeth. Her face was pale with dried sweat. She had on a single wrapper and a loose blouse. She caught his eye and came over to sell him some oranges. He didn't know how to refuse, so he bought two. When the girl went back to singing of her sweet oranges Joe felt something in him. The traffic eased. Joe smiled. Beneath his coat, he felt the quiet salute of desire.

He was tremulous with desperation when he got off the bus. He went to the bar in search of Sarah. She wasn't there. He ordered a few bottles of beer and he waited. The longer he waited the more unbearable his desire became. He suffered such an unabated hardness that he was forced to go home and change into his mud-spattered greatcoat. He went from one bar to another, hoping to find Sarah. He didn't find her. All night he was hard and it began to hurt in its hardness. He couldn't meditate, couldn't sleep. He tossed and turned, worried that the herbalist had given him an unusually strong dose of the antelope medicine. In the morning he was still hard. It was in the evening that he began to approach normality. And by then it had become clear that the only way he could find the Ghanian woman was through his friend, Cata-cata.

He chose an unfortunate time to pay a visit. When he knocked on the door and went in, he saw his friend's room in disarray. Clothes were scattered all over the bed.

On the cupboard there was a boxing glove that had been cut up grotesquely. There were torn photographs on the table. Cata-cata sat on a chair exhaling cigarette smoke like an enraged bull. He had scratches on his neck, and a cut on his forehead.

'What happened to you, my friend?'

'Nothing.'

'Nothing?'

'Woman problem, as usual.'

Joe laughed.

'What's so funny?'

'Nothing.'

They were silent, till Joe said: 'Did they beat you up again?'

'Who?'

'The women.'

'What women?'

'Nothing.'

'What women?'

'Forget it.'

Joe went and sat on the bed.

'Have you seen Sarah?'

'Why?'

'I want to talk to her.'

'Why?'

'Why not?'

'She's my woman.'

'What about the one you've got?'

'None of your business.'

'I want to talk to her.'

'About what?'

'About her brother, the one taking my course.'

'Leave her alone.'

'You're selfish.'

'Go and find your own woman, my friend.'

They were silent. Then Cata-cata put out his cigarette. He laughed.

'You should have seen those two big women fighting. They went at one another like hungry tigers. Fought and scratched. I hate women fighting, so I reconciled them. You know what I did afterwards, eh?'

'What?'

'I brought them home. And enjoyed both of them. Together.'

'Lie!' said Joe.

'True. I swear.'

'Lie!'

'How do you know it's a lie, eh? Were you there?'

'The Ghanian woman told me . . .'

'What . . .'

Cata-cata leapt up from the chair and rushed at Joe. He grabbed his friend by the collar of the greatcoat and shook him, wrenched him up, and threw him against the wall. Cata-cata went at him again, grabbed him round the neck, and pulled back his left fist. His eyes were deranged with jealousy. Then he suddenly relaxed. He lowered his fist. He went and sat down on the chair. He lit another cigarette. Neither of them spoke for a while. Joe stayed where he was with his back against the wall.

'I'm sorry, my friend.'

Joe was silent.

'Don't be angry. Me and my woman quarrelled before you arrived.'

Joe didn't move.

'So you are angry with me? Can't you forgive and forget? Okay. I will tell you where you can find her.'

Cata-cata told him; Joe still didn't speak. Cata-cata went out and bought three placatory bottles of beer: Joe continued with the sulky silence.

It was only when Cata-cata asked Joe to forget the money he owed, that Joe said: 'You don't know, and I won't tell you.'

He went to the door.

'Let's go fishing,' Cata-cata said.

'Tomorrow,' Joe said, shutting the door behind him.

They set out early in the morning on Saturday. Joe had cleaned out his room and sprinkled Dettol on the floor and over the walls. He had also been to the post office. He found four subscriptions to his course, paid for in postal orders. They set out with their fishing rods and tackles, their box of fish hooks, their jar of earthworms and insects. Cata-cata had brought some tangerines and oranges along with the three conciliatory bottles of beer. Not one word passed between them.

They caught two buses to get to FESTAC Estate along the Badagry road. Cata-cata had taken Joe fishing there before. The last time the short pier had been full of rubbish. When they arrived it was surprising for them to find the pier clean: it had been washed by the August rain.

It was a clear and hot day. The river water was brown and there were canoes in the distance. Crabs scuttled around the pier.

Joe lay flat on his back and watched the clear sky while Cata-cata fished.

'The fishes are asleep.'

'Maybe,' Joe said.

'Did I tell you about the dream I had last night, eh?'

'No.'

'I dreamt that I caught a fish, an electric fish, a big one. I clobbered it, but it wouldn't die. I threw a brick on its head, and do you know what happened, eh?'

'No.'

'The brick scattered into pieces. And the fish was crying. It wouldn't stop crying. In the end I threw the fish back into the river.'

'It's a good thing you did,' Joe said.

'I think so.'

'Do you want a beer?'

'No, but help yourself.'

Joe took a bottle. The beer was still chilled. He opened the bottle with his teeth and drank steadily through half of it. He burped. He looked across the river. On the other shore there were palm trees and huts. An eagle flew past low along the river.

Joe said: 'Too many competitors and not enough money.'

'True.'

'This life is a financial problem.'

'You're right.'

'But a man must fly.'

'A man is not a bird.'

Joe didn't say anything. He finished the bottle of beer.

'Did you go and see Sarah?'

'Yes.'

'What happened?'

'At first she didn't want to talk to me. Then we agreed to meet tonight.'

'I see.'

Joe looked across the river. He saw the trees against the sky. He saw the river softly rippling, softly flowing. He felt the wind cool beneath the warmth of the day. He felt peaceful. He was happy to see the crabs scuttling along the shore. He fell asleep and dreamt that he was paddling a canoe in a green bottle.

Then the midget with the big head and red eyes came to him and said: 'How are you?'

'I don't know. But how are you?'

'I am not feeling all that well.'

'What's wrong? Can I help?' Joe asked.

'Yes. I want you to give me back that thing I gave you. My life has been hell without it.'

'Please let me keep it. I will give you anything else you ask for.'

'If you want it, keep it.'

Joe didn't like the way the midget said that; so he gave the midget what he asked for.

'Thank you,' said the midget.

'Thank you,' said Joe.

'I am always happy to see you.'

'Thank you.'

'Don't thank me.'

'Okay. Tell me, what was that thing you gave me?'

'Bad luck,' the midget said, cheerfully.

'You are a true friend,' said Joe.

'So are you. Except for one thing. You've got your eyes always shut. Open them.'

Joe opened his eyes. Cata-cata was leaning over him.

'You've been talking in your sleep.'

'It's a small problem.'

'Have a tangerine.'

Joe peeled the tangerine and ate it. He felt light. He felt possessed of a secret wonder. The tangerine was cool in his mouth. He thought about prison. He thought about Sarah. He felt he had to turn off his thinking. He tried to, but he only succeeded in having an idea for his sixteenth lesson. He would call it: 'Turning Experience into Gold'.

He said: 'It's my birthday soon. Things will get better after my birthday.'

'Yes. Things might get better.'

'And then the rainy season continues.'

'Ponds everywhere. Mud everywhere.'
They stared at the river.
Joe said: 'This life of mine has been one long fever.
Now I feel I'm getting well.'
'That's good. That's good,' his friend said, smiling.